About the Author

I am a retired obstetrician who composed this story thirty years ago and now revised it.

Doctor Zangonini's Dog

M. Z. Graysar

Doctor Zangonini's Dog

Olympia Publishers
London

www.olympiapublishers.com
OLYMPIA PAPERBACK EDITION

Copyright © M. Z. Graysar 2024

The right of M. Z. Graysar to be identified as author of
this work has been asserted in accordance with sections 77 and 78 of
the Copyright, Designs and Patents Act 1988.

All Rights Reserved

No reproduction, copy or transmission of this publication
may be made without written permission.
No paragraph of this publication may be reproduced,
copied or transmitted save with the written permission of the publisher,
or in accordance with the provisions
of the Copyright Act 1956 (as amended).

Any person who commits any unauthorised act in relation to
this publication may be liable to criminal
prosecution and civil claims for damage.

A CIP catalogue record for this title is
available from the British Library.

ISBN: 978-1-80439-662-9

This is a work of fiction.
Names, characters, places and incidents originate from the writer's
imagination. Any resemblance to actual persons, living or dead, is
purely coincidental.

First Published in 2024

**Olympia Publishers
Tallis House
2 Tallis Street
London
EC4Y 0AB**

Printed in Great Britain

CHAPTER 1

John opened his slumbering eyes and reluctantly moved his eyelids upward to face the new day. Early morning sunshine had burst into the room and illuminated it.

The warm and dry air was awash with the sound of chirping birds. A faint blow of wind forced the air through the double hung window and refreshed the room air, a prelude to a nice late June day.

John moved out of the bed and stood by the window.

His feeling of freshness and crispness was the testimony of a night well rested and not awakened by the hospital or one of his patients.

The ancient oak tree visible through the window was exhibiting its lush green leaves with their morning dew, which glittered under the bright sunshine, as if a proud pearl fisher was showing his freshly acquired treasure on the palm of his hand.

The view made the corners of his lips move upwards. He was proud of his old tree, whose age in his estimate easily surpassed a hundred. The memories of its shade offering a retreat from the summer heat when he was mowing the lawn rested in the comfort zone of his mind.

The lawn on his front yard was separated from the street by a walkway and a line of tall trees which flanked both sides of the street. The walkway intensified his longing to go for a walk, enjoy the fresh air, look at the robins busy picking into the grass in search of worms, the squirrel scurrying to climb a tree or hide behind one whenever he passed by. It was always a source of enjoyment for him.

He had to stifle his yearning for a walk. Lucy's operation was scheduled at seven thirty a.m.

Lucy was a slender woman of average proportion. Her brown hair was parted in the middle and reached her shoulder.

Two ocean blue eyes transmitted calm, and whenever her frequent smiles adorned her face, two rows of pearl white teeth enhanced her charm.

They met the first time in John's office where she had come for a consultation for her six-week-old pregnancy.

The blood stain on her underpants when she woke up in the morning reminded her of a girlfriend who found a blood speck on her pants, and had ended up with a miscarriage.

John's secretary had a hard time to calm the petrified woman. She squeezed her into the top of her schedule as an emergency.

When John entered the room, he faced two blue eyes projecting worry and concern.

He was about to say hi when the quiet of the room was broken by a quivering voice.

"Hi, I am Lucy and I moved to this neighborhood last week."

And John answered, "Hi, I am Dr. Zangonini. How can I help you?

Lucy, while trying hard to infuse some calmness into her voice, continued, "When I woke up this morning, my underpants were stained with a blood spot."

She paused, her eyes staring at John, giving away her fear.

It took few seconds before she could continue. "I am here to ask you, is my kid OK? Will I be able to hold him in my arms and press my lips against his cheek?" Her voice was hardly audible.

Dr. Zangonini, in an effort to calm her down, put his hand on her shoulder and glanced at her reassuringly, and said, "Let me first take your history and check you; afterwards, we will have plenty of time to talk about it."

Lucy could hardly wait for the end of the exam. Her fearful eyes followed every move of John.

John got off his examining stool, pushed back the stirrups and helped her to an upright position. Then he pressed her shoulder gently, and uttered in a turned-down voice, "Don't worry everything is ok." The statement tranquilized her, as seen on her relaxing face, but her two blue eyes were piercing into John's face for an explanation.

John continued with the same voice, "Don't worry, the source of your spotting is from outside the womb, which we call the cervix, and has nothing to do with the inside, where the pregnancy is located. Your baby is OK." The test results corroborated his statement.

After eight months of an uneventful pregnancy, baby Brian's picture was taken, with his overjoyed mother holding him in her chest, pressing her lips against his cheek and Dr. Zangonini standing at the bedside in his scrub suit, by her husband, Robert.

Lucy lived in the same neighborhood; she and John crossed paths often in the quarter they shared and engaged in casual conversation.

At one occasion, his glance at Brian prompted the words, "He looks so pretty." He lifted him up. Throwing him up in the air brought a big smile to Lucy's face, exhibiting her pearl white teeth. While Brian's giggle vibrated in the air, John's lips pressed against Brian's cheek.

Her annual exam filled John with concern. Lucy's cheerful face was directed toward John, expecting the good news as usual.

When she was confronted with John's serious face, her reaction was immediate.

"Is everything OK?" was the sentence which jumped out of her mouth before John had a chance to explain his findings.

After few seconds of staring at her, he announced, with a voice clearly struggling to overcome his concern, "Your exam is not quite normal."

A terrified face looked at John for a moment. The words coming out of her mouth were hardly audible. "What do you mean by 'quite normal'?"

"There is a cystic mass the size of a grapefruit on the left side of your pelvis," he responded.

It took a while for her to stop staring at John and move her lips. "Level with me. Does it mean I have cancer?

"I don't think so. The surface of the tumor is very smooth and it is freely moveable; these are good signs, they speak against a cancerous tumor," he responded.

He grabbed her upper arm and squeezed it gently, and said, "It has to come out. I will order some tests, but the exam of the specimen by the pathologist who receives it after the removal will be the final word." The ultrasound test corroborated his findings.

The operation was scheduled for seven thirty a.m. and John had to scratch his daily walk from his routine in order to be on time.

CHAPTER 2

During his drive to the hospital, his mind was struggling to find a way to explain it to her, in case the mass turned out to be malignant.

When he entered the operating room, the anesthesiologist was preparing the injection to put her to sleep. Despite his mask and the scrub suit, Lucy had recognized him immediately, as the folds on her eye corners attested a happy face.

John approached her, pressed her arm rather firmly and said in a reassuring tone, "Don't worry, everything is going to be OK." Lucy dropped her eyelids, signaling her acceptance.

The scalpel moved fast in John's hand; soon, the abdomen was open, and John was exploring it. The tumor's surface was smooth and free of any outgrows, which was very reassuring to John. It was removed and sent to the pathologist for a frozen section exam, i.e. the pathologist will make a slide and, after examining it microscopically, convey his diagnosis to the surgeon.

John was busy working on her when the silence of the operating room was shattered by the ringing of the phone. The circulating nurse lifted up the receiver and, after few seconds of listening, brought it to John and put it on his ear.

"It is the pathologist," she said.

The tumor was benign, he had announced. The sigh of relief jumping out of John's mouth was loud enough to be heard by the anesthesiologist.

He knew well enough that it wasn't of his making, but he would have loved to use it as a feather on his cap.

Lucy was faintly awake when she was brought to the recovery room.

Her beaming face was testimony to her joy, after hearing John announcing that the tumor was noncancerous. The kiss placed on her cheek by her husband, Robert, signaled the end of their anxiety.

Back at home, a relaxed John was sitting on the couch reflecting on what to do with the rest of the day. Lucy was the only case scheduled for his otherwise busy operating day.

The sunshine brightening the room intensified his longing for a walk. The walkways, as he could see through the large window of the living room, were empty, short of the occasional solo stroller.

The manicured lawns, with rhododendron bushes on their border, always grabbed his attention when walking. Red color pleased his eyes all the time. The crowns of the tall maple, elm and oak trees flanking the street were so wide that some were entangled with the opposite tree, allowing very little sunshine to go through. He lifted his head to look at the ceiling created by the tree crowns. The sunshine shimmered through the leaves and made them appear like stained glasses of a cathedral. For few seconds, he sensed the vibration of Bach's cantata in his ears, as if he was lost in a church. He raised his right hand to touch his neck due to some tingling he was feeling and noticed the skin of his neck was not smooth. The immediate palpation of the area caught a tiny mass, the size of a lentil between his fingertips.

Adjacent to the mass, there were two smaller bumps interrupting the smoothness of the skin. The thought of an infection in his throat that had spread out to the lymph glands on his neck hit his mind. He had to abandon it quickly, for his memory was void of any recent infection of his mouth or throat.

A bug bite was the easy explanation, especially if one spends a lot of time outside, though he never felt any itching in that region. On the way back home, he was enjoying the lawn and bushes, while his right hand kept palpating his neck, something he wasn't even aware of. Were it not for the familiar front porch of his house, which he bought thirty years ago, he would have passed it.

Once he entered the house, he stepped immediately toward the mirror in the foyer. The skin of his neck in the mirror looked as smooth as always. He avoided palpating his neck and headed toward the kitchen, where he prepared his brown mug of coffee.

Relaxing in the patio with coffee was a good idea, he thought.

The shade thrown on the patio by the maple tree covered a big spot, where four chairs were arranged around a round table. A moment after his behind had touched the chair looking at the trees, his thoughts were interrupted by a familiar-sounding voice. It was Jane, who was back home. For Jane, it was unexpected to see John at home so soon.

"Are you already done? It is a big surprise to see you when I return from school."

"Well, today I had a very light schedule; Lucy was the only one," he responded, and went on, "As you see, I am relaxing."

She used to lie down after school, for ten to fifteen minutes. It gave her tranquility and made up for the stress of the school. Today, after gazing at John, she uttered, "The sight of you in the patio sipping coffee is so inviting that I am going to make a black tea and join you."

Few minutes passed before she approached the patio,

holding a steaming mug with the string of a tea bag hanging over the edge of the mug. Her steps were short and slow. She put the mug on the table, her derriere occupying the chair facing his. After a moment of glancing at John, her lips moved, "Last night, you expressed your concern for your case of today, and I guess the way everything turned out, satisfied you. You are sitting here very relaxed, am I correct?"

A pleasant surprise loaded John's face. He didn't expect that last night's brief mention of Lucy's tumor and the possibility it could be cancerous would linger on Jane's memory. The corners of his lips moved upwards and his eyes glittered when he answered her question. "I was very content with the result." He continued, "I went for a walk when I returned, the fresh air had cleared my lungs faster. Now I am relaxing on the patio, as you see."

Jane nodded while her eyes followed his right hand, moving again toward his neck and palpating it. She had never observed it before, a phenomenon completely new to her. Her staring at his neck continued for a brief moment. At the end of the day, she gave in to her curiosity and asked John, "Why are you touching your neck again and again?"

His puzzled glance at her lasted few seconds before he was able to answer. "I wasn't aware I was touching my neck. I have a bug bite in my neck and probably the tingling in my neck moved my hand toward it, and didn't attract my attention."

To come home and unexpectedly encounter John, who was done with his routine and was waiting for her, put her in a festive mood. The thought of going out for dinner took over her mind, but it changed quickly when she passed through the kitchen with the refrigerator full of groceries she had bought yesterday. No restaurant can beat her delicious food she will prepare, she thought.

She sautéed spinach and mixed it with beaten eggs and her special herbs, grilled fresh salmon and put it on top of it. Her specialty sauce poured over the salmon completed the dish.

The silverware on white napkins glittered under the kitchen light. John took the seat across from Jane and opened a bottle of Beaujolais.

Two glasses filled with red wine up to one inch to the rim were raised and they toasted to each other's health. The bite of dish moved his eyelids down and filled his face with pleasant satisfaction. His lips didn't wait for the bite to go down and moved to announce how delicious it was.

John kept watching her blue eyes as if he was seeing them for the first time. They were adorned with long lashes, thickened with mascara and twinkled with special charm. Her flaxen hair, bushy and shiny, bobbed at the middle of her neck, and two rows of pearl white teeth appeared now and then when she was chewing the salmon.

He recalled her out of shape body when she was pregnant, but she regained her slender body fast. Her muscles were in a hurry to follow suit and became firm again, making it easy to fit into her jeans. People frequently mistook her tall and handsome seventeen-year-old son, Josh, for her brother. John continued glancing at her again and again while sipping more wine. Jane stared at John and finally opened her mouth and uttered, "Is everything OK with my face? Perhaps I should refresh my makeup?

"Not at all," was John's response. "Your face and your body are as enchanting as twenty years ago, when I met you for the first time, and the desire to seduce you to the bedroom is creeping all over me."

A shy smile brightening her face was all her answer.

In the bedroom, he lit a one-foot-long citron candle. A sweet aroma gradually filled up the air. A third glass of Beaujolais was flooding John's blood and boosted the prickling of his skin.

In bed and naked, he grabbed her left breast, which was as firm as before her pregnancy. He cupped his hand around her butt; the transmission of firmness into his system was very pleasant and they hugged. They chewed each other's lips gently, while her hand caressed the nape of his neck, and ran through her hair. They embraced again, and she kissed the top of his nose and upper lip. The warmth of her breath caressed his skin and made him feel so light, as if he was a feather and was floating in the air. He pressed his chest against hers and ran his lips over her body.

They joined and became one.

They were lying beside each other, relaxed and quiet. All their worries were banished to the realm of oblivion. John's memory of the bug bite vanished, as if it never existed.

CHAPTER THREE

The early morning sunshine was unusually bright, a big welcome for John, who got up and stood in front of the window, admiring his ancient oak tree.

The bathroom was not illuminated that much, so he turned on the light switch.

Standing in front of the mirror, looking at his reflection, gave him a sense of complacency. A full head of black hair made the occasional gray insignificant. A shadow of a wrinkle ran from the side of his nostril to the corner of his lip. The hints of crow feet on the corners of his eyes made him move fast to search for other possible wrinkles, which he couldn't find. Not bad for a fifty-one-year-old guy, he thought.

While he was enjoying his image in the mirror, something in his mouth started to taste differently. He moved his tongue and the metallic taste intensified, and he spit into the sink, and as if struck by lightning, he froze. There was blood in the saliva. His eyes were fixed at the sink. It enlivened the memory of the bug bite. He raised his right hand and palpated the right side of his neck. The bug bite was still there, maybe a little bigger. His primordial fear of bugs made him dodge his head when he heard the buzzing of a bee. It turned out the buzzing was an auditory hallucination brought about by his fear of bees.

He didn't wash up the blood-tinged sputum, since he was looking for the source of blood. A meticulous scrutiny of his mouth revealed a normal tongue and mouth.

The scenario taking shape in his mind was so upsetting that he tried to delete it from his mind, without success.

A tumor in his upper throat was growing and ulcerating, causing the blood to flow into his mouth and giving him the metallic taste, and the cells of the tumor were wandering to other part of the body, and the first place to settle down were the lymph glands of the upper neck. That is where he was feeling the bug bite. A terrible thought, but at least he had found an explanation for the little mass on his neck, just a resting place for cancer cells to reproduce and invade the other organs. He was a doctor, and he knew how cancer cells behaved.

His glance was fixed at the bloody sputum for few more seconds before he washed it off the sink. For a while, he was wondering where the noise was coming from; his mind was preoccupied with the consequences of cancer with his professional life. It took him a few moments to realize he had to close the faucet.

He took refuge on the chair in the bedroom, trying to pour oil on troubled waters.

CHAPTER FOUR

Today was Wednesday, his day off, when the routine meeting for lunch with Dr. Martin was on his schedule.

Martin, a dear friend from his medical school days, was now an accomplished general surgeon. The meeting worked well to offset the stresses of the week.

His new theory for his bug bite had made his mind more preoccupied with cancer than to see Martin for lunch. It took a long time for John to decide to take the bull by the horns and cancel the meeting. He thought he was saving Martin from a lackluster conversation and a boring meeting. He was searching for a reason to cancel it. The lack of appetite which he was experiencing was not good enough for an excuse, he thought. His preoccupation with cancer and being absent-minded in the meeting were his real reasons, but Martin shouldn't be involved in his problems, John's mind wasn't ready for it. After few minutes of thought about Martin's unobtrusive character, he grabbed the phone and called his number.

"Hi, this is Martin," the voice on the other side of the line announced.

"Hi, this is John. I have to cancel our lunch meeting. I don't feel well," he responded without being able to hide the tinge of sadness in his voice.

Martin realized immediately that John wanted to be alone and responded, "I hope you will feel well soon. Don't hesitate to call me if I could be of any help."

John responded, "Thank you, I will, and I am looking forward to our next lunch meeting," and hung up.

John was happy Martin was not intrusive and didn't want to dig any further about his wellbeing.

CHAPTER FIVE

The couch in the living room offered him, as usual, a spot to lie down, relax and contemplate. Though he was trying hard, he couldn't stop the images of his former patients who had succumbed to cancer, passing by him some with a big smile on their face, as if implying 'see you soon'. Seemingly, his deep layer of subconscious where he had stored them had become active again. Maybe Jane should be let in and that will reduce his concerns, he thought, though it was something his mind still wasn't ready to accept. It was the ringing of the doorbell which disrupted the chain of his thoughts.

When he opened the door, the mailman with a big smile greeted him and handed him the special delivery. It was a packet for his wife.

His back pressing the couch's sitting area, his glance fixed at the ceiling, he started reflecting on his future.

The premonition that he had to pull up the stakes and put an end to his practice was overwhelming. It took him many minutes to arrive at a decision. He will close down temporarily and dedicate his time to work up and treat his tumor. What came afterwards was in the laps of gods.

He woke up early in the morning; the blue sky was void of clouds and the sun added a pleasant warmth to the air, which enhanced the enticement for an early walk in him. An early walk will enable him to make his hospital rounds and finish his office, even though it could be his last time, may be the swan song of his professional life.

He stepped out of the house for his early walk. Jane was in sound sleep when he returned the night before; her alarm was set to go off thirty minutes earlier than usual. When he arrived, she was already gone, so he headed toward the shower.

To his astonishment, the hot shower set his mind free of concern, and increased his feeling of being hungry.

He pleased his stomach with cereal mixed with milk and raisin, and headed toward the hospital. Luckily, the two patients to be seen were ready for discharge. The short conversation with a colleague on his way out delayed him for few minutes, but his office started in the late afternoon anyway.

Dr. Logan was the one who covered for him in case of his absence and vice versa. John's mind was preoccupied to find the reasons for asking him for a longer period of coverage. The dusk was setting in and he was finished with his office. Finally, he had decided to say the real reason he wanted coverage, which was his health. He informed his office personnel that the office will stay closed until he feels OK again, and called Dr. Logan. Although he was happy Logan didn't ask about details of his disease, nevertheless the urge to talk about it with someone was sweeping him off his feet.

When he was back, it was already after nine p.m., and he went upstairs to the bedroom to check on Jane. She was already in the arms of Morpheus. He stepped down and walked toward the kitchen. A plate of basmati rice and cherry tomatoes was looking at him. On top of the rice sat a piece of grilled chicken breast and the sauce's appearance betrayed its origin from chutney. The plate had become cold, but the microwave oven was just a few steps away.

John's taste buds were so gratified with the food, they made him thank Jane in absentia. John's preparation to get to bed was shorter than usual. He was in a hurry to get to bed and spread himself like an eagle, his favorite position. The thought that the posture wouldn't stop his throat tumor from further mushrooming had not entered his mind.

CHAPTER SIX

The cloudy day augmented the darkness in the room. Jane's side of the bed was empty, revealing Jane's quiet departure. She never disturbed John in his sleep, since she never knew when he got into his bed.

John, though sure about a tumor in his throat, was aware that he had to verify it by x-ray.

His dream was still lingering in his brain. His MRI had shown his throat to be clear. The thought made the corners of his lips move toward the north when he pulled over the phone from the nightstand and dialed Jim's number. Jim was the head of radiology, and they maintained a friendly relationship, so he was able to schedule his MRI of head and neck for the same day.

The cheerful young technician adjusted his head into the machine and gave him the necessary instructions. The calmness and quiet flowing out of her were contagious. John closed his eyes to ignore the machine noise and maintain the new peacefulness.

He had ignored the grumbling of his stomach, which usually directed him toward doctor's lounge, where he always satisfied his feeling of hunger. Instead, he found himself in obstetrics/gynecology ward, after he had finished his MRI. *Well, old habits die hard*, he thought, with a smile on his face.

He headed to doctor's lounge while in his head the idea of

an intruder who had taken residence in his throat and was about to enter other parts of his body was brooding.

The lounge, save for a doctor who was sunk in his lazy chair and was half concealed behind the newspaper he was absorbed in, was empty of individuals. Food and coffee maker were visible on the counter at the west end of the lounge.

The colorful exhibition of fresh fruits, nuts and sliced bread on the counter invited to sample them even if you were not hungry. John's sandwich, made out of sliced turkey, tomato and green vegetables, turned out to be delicious, and the added caffeine gave him enough perk to walk to the parking lot

It was eight p.m. and dark when he was back home. He could see well when he entered the kitchen, because the adjacent living room was illuminated. The red wine glittered in the glass which he had filled to the rim; it was from his last Malbec bottle. By the time his heavy steps took him to the bedroom, more than half of the bottle was circulating in his blood, apparently not enough to obscure the thought of cancer in his mind. He didn't know when Jane would be back from her meeting and he was already in his pajamas, so he stretched himself in the bed. With his eyes closed, he tried to draw a picture for his future. In a matter of a few minutes, he succumbed to slumber and got lost in the darkness.

After breakfast the next morning, he was sitting in his living room couch with his eyes fixed at the phone, just dialing the radiology number plus his code would enable him to listen to the result of his MRI. A thought he had to wrestle with, since, in his mind, the cancer had already a firm spot. But the idea of oncologists insisting on a diagnosis i.e. to have the x-ray result and have it biopsied, was something he was totally aware of. His eyes moved toward the phone and his right arm was about to grab it when his second thoughts overwhelmed him. What if it wasn't cancer and it was just a swelling due to a viral infection? Needless to say, the idea made his lips move upwards. It took a few steps of walking up and down the living room to evaporate his wishful thinking. He returned to the couch and perched on it. Just few more moments of uncertainty and he overcame his hesitation and grabbed the phone.

The results interpreted by the radiologist pointed to a tumor sitting in the throat with three metastatic lymph nodes on the neck, a result he was expecting, but he didn't anticipate the sound in his ears which was like a bombshell.

He had to swallow it, though back in his mind a shimmer of hope, no matter how small, that the treatment would have some success was glittering. At the end of the day, he was pleased with his decision to arrange coverage for his practice.

The brutal force of nature obliges you to actions you never thought would be necessary.

The time was ripe to biopsy the tumor and establish the diagnosis and the nature of the tumor, something the oncologist and the radiation therapist will insist upon. He knew Dr. Martin would be a suitable person for the job. However to call Martin, his dear friend, looked to him as a challenge. He had called him recently and cancelled their lunch meeting on the ground of not feeling well; now to call and ask him for a sampling of his tumor will reveal his real reason for cancelling, and maybe Martin's mind would consider him a dishonest man. To avoid this prospect, he thought to appear in person and explain his situation. Without any hesitation, he grabbed the phone and called Martin's office.

The receptionist of Dr. Martin put him down as the sixth patient on the schedule as John Zangonini.

Dr. Martin stepped in his examining room. "Hi," slipped out of his mouth automatically and was about to continue when his eyes met John's face, his mouth stayed half open and he was speechless; his eyes were staring at John and his face was dumbfounded.

John realized right away his role in creating the situation and tried to fine tune his words for explaining the circumstances.

"Sorry, I should have notified you of my throat tumor at the time of cancellation the lunch meeting," he uttered. Martin continued staring at him and John continued, "I didn't want to discuss my tumor over the phone."

It took a while for Dr. Martin to regain his composure. His face turned into a welcoming one and out of his mouth came the words, "What kind of biopsy are you talking about, can you be more specific?" A sign he was deaf to John's statement of his throat tumor when John's presence in his examining room had taken him by surprise.

John squarely looked into his eyes and responded, with a solemn voice, "You recall that I cancelled our lunch meeting on the ground of not feeling well." He tossed a glance at Martin's face, as if he was studying it. Martin's eyes were indicating more questions. "Well, I had found out that my throat was inflicted with a disease which has turned out to be a tumor. All clinical findings, including the x-ray, suggest a cancerous tumor. I am trying to confirm it by a biopsy, which will aid the radiation therapist and the oncologist, too."

The lines of Martin's face were showing optimism and hopefulness before he moved his lips to utter his feelings. "Your dark days ahead will throw a shadow on your life, but I see the silver lining: your treatment will be successful, and you will return back to work sooner than you think."

John and Martin hugged each other. Martin's right arm was wrapped around John's shoulder and his face was directed toward John with two eyes glittering with hope when they said goodbye.

CHAPTER SEVEN

A haziness of the air blurred the sunset and soon the gradual disappearance of gabled roofs announced the dusk and following darkness. It was the day after the biopsy and John was on his way home. A ray of hope was penetrating into the darkness of his thoughts: 'The biopsy result had shown a benign-noncancerous-tumor and all he had to do was to remove it and his ordeal will vanish'. He was certainly as entitled to wishful thinking as the others.

The smell of freshly brewed coffee greeted his olfactory senses when he entered his house. Jane was preparing the coffee in the kitchen. A big smile occupied her face on seeing John. She embraced him, pursed her lips and pressed them against his cheek.

"Hi, John, I am glad you are done; now we can enjoy the coffee together and relax." John caressed her hair and kissed it. He was attempting to avoid saying much, lest the gloom in his thoughts tinge whatever he said.

John was enjoying his coffee, which always perked him up, however it wasn't enough to concoct a phrase to convey to her that a tumor in his throat had stopped him to practice his profession. The sound of the ringing phone put an end to the brooding in his head.

"Hi, John, how are you". To discern the voice on the phone as Martin's was simple.

"Hi, Martin, I am doing fine, what is up?" was his response.

"I have the result of the biopsy," Martin announced.

"Oh, nice, I didn't expect it so soon," he answered.

"Well, I left the pathologist a message to inform me as soon as it was available." Martin sounded calm on the phone and, to follow, his silence was upsetting for John. It took Martin a while before he continued.

"It is a nasopharyngeal cancer," he continued without waiting for John's response or reaction. "At this point, my duty as your surgeon should end, but I can't take off the load of obligation our friendship puts on my shoulder. I called the oncologist, Dr. Levinson, and discussed your case with him and forwarded copies of your findings to him. I think you will be in good hands, and I hope you don't think I have gone too far."

John's response was with a voice not showing a hint of his disappointment, although by now the hope that the tumor might be benign should have left his mind.

"I appreciate all you have done for me and will make an appointment with Dr. Levinson as soon as possible. Let me reinstate, my thankfulness to you is without boundaries, and I am looking forward to our next lunch meeting where I can hug you again".

The biopsy results not only confirmed his fears but also made him ready for his imminent battle with his infliction. The chemotherapy and radiation would be more bearable with having Jane as his partner. Her chest would offer comfort when nausea and vomiting attack him, and she will increase the liquid amounts in her delicacies to offset his reduced saliva.

The phrase which will convey to Jane his cancer was still escaping his mind. Jane was not allowed to participate in his concerns from the beginning, and to prepare her for the big shock now seemed to represent a big challenge.

Meanwhile Jane had moved to the patio with a mug of coffee in hand. The patio chair offered her a spot to perch and unwind. The quiet of the patio was enhanced by the arrival of the dusk and she didn't disturb it by turning on the patio light. The occasional rustle in the maple tree of the back yard augmented the relaxing atmosphere.

John joined Jane in the patio. His rear end occupied the chair across from Jane, and he had decided on doing his revelation of having been inflicted with cancer cold turkey.

His silent look at Jane triggered the question by Jane: "Are you OK? You are staring at me with gloomy eyes without mentioning a word."

John looked at her with indifference, as if he was still lost in his thoughts, and responded, "I am fine. Sometimes the breaking of dusk puts me in a sad mood."

Years of togetherness had given Jane the opportunity to explore the corners and niches of John's soul and it wasn't hard for her to discern that John's sad mood was not related to the setting of dusk.

Questions she was asking herself were pertinent and intensified her longing for an honest answer. *Is there something he is hiding from me? Is there a secret he doesn't want to share with me?*

Her eyes were piercing John's face in obvious disbelief, and it took her almost a full minute before her lips moved and out came a solemn voice, uttering, "Are you hiding something from me?"

For John, the question was mind-shattering, for he was indeed hiding his fears behind the bug bite, yet he had made the decision to reveal that it was cancer. Tossing a normal look at Jane to hide his fears, he stated, "You remember, a few days ago, you asked me why I was so frequently touching my neck?"

Jane's puzzled look betrayed her forgetting of the matter. She opened her mouth and uttered, "So, what about it?"

"Well, I told you it was a bug bite," he stated.

The premonition of something bad embraced Jane. She was trying to analyze the implications of his inquiry about a bug bite. The analysis of the bug bite didn't throw any light on the matter and she asked herself, *why isn't he giving me a straight answer?* It wasn't the curiosity but the premonition of a disease presenting as a bug bite which made her look at John's face and utter, "What is your point about the bug bite?"

John stared at Jane's face for a few seconds before a voice devoid of any emotion vibrated the air. "Well, the bug bite was biopsied, and it turned out to be cancer".

Jane's face was deprived of any expression and was directed at John's. The blinking of her eyes stopped and her speech abandoned her.

The wetness in her eyes were increasing with every passing moment. It took a short time for the first drop of tear to appear on the corners of her eyes and roll along her nose to her lips.

She slowly got up off her chair and approached John, extended her arms around John's shoulder and pressed her cheek against his. They tightened their hug with every passing second, as if struggling to prevent the evil to separate them.

CHAPTER EIGHT

Dr. Levinson's office was located in the professional building a few steps away from the hospital. In his appointment book, John was listed as the seventh patient. In his effort to avoid favoritism, he had called the office and made an appointment as John Zangonini, a cancer patient, and deliberately eschewed the doctor title.

Levinson was in his middle age, with a black moustache which did a good job to conceal a lip scar, a remnant of a previous surgery. His black hair was thinning; finding a gray one required a second look. Behind his metal framed glasses, two brown eyes registered the images of his patients. The most salient part of him was his stooped neck and back, which deducted four inches from his six feet statue.

John had referred patients to him, who were very content with his bedside manner. His ability to satisfy patients was known and was a characteristic well-regarded among referring staff members.

In addition to the receptionist, two skilled nurse oncologists called his office their working place. The office possessed all the facilities to qualify as an outpatient oncology treatment center.

Two discrete rooms, each appointed with an examining table and a lazy chair, a comfortable place to rest and pass the time of chemotherapy.

On sunny days, a silvery sunshine covered the shelves which were fastened to the wall. A slew of medications could be found in alphabetical order on the shelves. A brass plate attached to the doors of each room read: treatment center. The only way to enter the treatment center was through the waiting area. On opening the door from the waiting room, one was greeted with the brass signs.

John came earlier than he was expected, and was taken by surprise when he was confronted by so many patients waiting. He was seventh on the list, but at least twenty pairs of eyes moved toward him when he entered the room. A guy who was sunken behind his newspaper before John's arrival threw a glance at John with a grin easy to interpret: 'Welcome to the league.'

John's derriere touched the seat, and he was scrutinizing the waiting patients when the door to the treatment room opened. The scene grabbed immediately his attention. A young man, his one hand holding on to his IV stand, was walking toward the toilette as if nobody was present in the room. The man was in his twenties, scarce brownish hair attached to his head, which was carried by an emaciated body. His cheeks were sunken deeply, exposing his upper jawbone. John quickly changed the direction of his eyes, as if lingering on him wouldn't let him prevent the same fate.

The receptionist opened the door of Levinson's consultation room. The palm of her hand was keeping the door open and John's name echoed in the air. John entered the room and shook hand with Levinson.

"You didn't have to make an appointment, I could have accommodated you, as you know it."

John answered with a smile on his face, "It is OK, let's get to the point," he responded.

Dr. Levinson's response started with a smile too. "Well, Dr. Martin has discussed your case with me and forwarded to me all the documents, so I am very well informed about your disease. The type of tumor you have is vulnerable to radiation and chemotherapy, and as far as I know, they work best if they go hand in hand. Of course, we will stop the chemo if your body shows weakness, and restart it when it has regained its strength." The discussion of the treatment took quite some time and John knew he had come for treatment and signed the consent.

The day he entered the treatment room, he was greeted by a heavyset woman who presented herself as Anne and directed him to the lazy chair, which was situated beside the window. The view of the blue sky, devoid of any cloud, made him calm.

    He made himself comfortable on the lazy chair. His eyes threw a glance at the IV stand the nurse brought to his side and immediately were glued to the plastic bottle with his name on it. He felt a shuddering in his spine. The poison will soon circulate in his blood, killing all fast-dividing cells of his bone marrow and making him defenseless against infections. The nurse approached him with a smile and announced, "Now I am going to attach it to your vein and let it circulate in your blood, and don't let it damage your bone marrow, I want to see you again next week." She was doing her job according to the standards of care and wasn't aware of her lack of compassion. A bigger smile widened her mouth when she knew of John's following radiation treatment. "I see you are having a double whammy today, don't forget your radiation." John nodded with a grin on his face.

    John headed toward the radiation center. He knew his appointment was forty minutes later and the radiation center was just ten minutes' walking distance from the chemo treatment. He had almost one hour until his next appointment, but his curiosity to scrutinize the waiting patients took hold of him and he headed toward the radiation center.

A total surprise hit him when he entered the waiting room of the radiotherapy. The room was almost empty, except for a gray-haired woman in her sixties who was totally absorbed in reading her leather-bound book.

John perched across from the woman and said, "Hi."

She didn't even lift her head when in response the word hi came out of her mouth.

John was very curious to find out the title of the book, which had engrossed the two large eyes behind the frameless glasses. His stealthy looks with the corners of his eyes were not successful. Instead, they must have alerted the woman somehow, since she turned her head toward John with a big smile and started reading from the book. "Be strong and courageous. Don't be afraid and discouraged, for the lord, your god is with you wherever you go."

She was interrupted by a young woman, who had opened the door and called, "Miss Garner, come in, please," looking straight toward the woman.

Miss Garner turned to John and said, "You can go in first, I want to finish reading this page."

The radiation, including the preparation, took only few minutes, longer than introduction of the young lady.

The sun's last slice had almost disappeared, heralding the darkening of the world when he returned home. The darkness was complete now. He recalled his aimless driving after his radiation, and seeing the images of the young man holding on to his IV stand, asking himself, was he going toward the same condition?

He was glad to be back home where he could talk with Jane about the events of the day. It was dark now, and he moved toward the living room and announced, "Honey, I am back," which didn't trigger a response.

In the bedroom, he found Jane possessed by slumber, though it was shortly after eight. The bottle of pills on the nightstand was the article which needed immediate investigation. He grabbed the bottle and counted the pills; only one was missing. The sigh of relief calmed him. The thought that she had to forgo dinner and a sleeping pill had to dissolve in her blood stream to make her forget the evil which had entered their life disturbed him so much that he felt paralyzed and had to lie down. He tried to analyze the reasons why the cancer found its way to his body.

His eyes were fixed at the images appearing in the ceiling. They were adding life to this planet; it was stressful, no matter if it was the daytime or he was pulled out of the bed. The numerous times he was called to help reduce the suffering of an individual were full of stress, enough to cause some cells in his body to go awry and become cancerous.

It was an easy way to settle on frequent stressful situations which made his body weak and subject to cancer attack. It didn't take long to realize that the taxing situations his thoughts were preoccupied with were part of his job, and it was ridiculous that it entered his mind.

Meanwhile, his efforts continued looking for a culprit for his cancer. All of a sudden, he saw the sun shining on the sky, with tall trees and greeneries everywhere. He couldn't discern if he was dreaming or hallucinating; nevertheless, it had attracted the focus of his attention.

The pasture allowed a herd of zebras to graze in tranquility. The roaring of a lion broke the quietness of the place. Its galloping signaled the imminent danger of annihilation and the entire herd began to run as fast as they could. A baby zebra couldn't keep up with his mother and soon fell prey to the lion, who nipped him by the neck. Seconds later, the lifeless body of the baby zebra was dangling from the lion's mouth, who was carrying him to a secure place to enjoy his lunch. John's attention was diverted to the random act of nature, and he thought he had the answer. The baby zebra's weakness to keep up with his mother became his fate. At the end of the day, he had hit the nail on the head and had the right answer.

He closed his eyes to coordinate his conclusion with his condition. That is when the thought crept into his mind and made his lips become like a crescent. He was recalling how excessive he was in pleasing his sweet tooth, with tons of whipped cream poured over fresh red berries.

It gratified his taste for the sweet, but also weakened his throat cells.

He turned around and incidentally his glance hit Jane's face.

For a while, he thought he saw a sardonic grin on her face, which made him quickly abandon his ideas.

John hadn't given up why he was chosen to provide domicile to a daemon in his throat.

His pondering brought him back to his youth, when he was in medical school.

CHAPTER NINE

He remembered the day he was assigned a case to write about.

He had gotten up early and was standing in front of the window, admiring the big trees with their numerous branches. It was late fall and most of their leaves were turning yellow, some lying on the ground, some already dried up.

The thick clouds had buried the sun, making it a gloomy day. John finished his breakfast and got on his way to the hospital.

The strong wind blowing from the south made the branches move in a wild way. Some young trees with thinner trunks looked like they were about to be uprooted. The wind was not only strong but also so cold; John felt it not only on his skin, but it pierced through his bones, reminding him of the cold winter ahead.

John was on his way from medical school to the hospital's children's department. The way was heavy with dried up fall leaves crunching under his steps. The noise didn't distract his mind from being preoccupied with his clinical assignment, meaning to see a patient, take her or his clinical history, examine her or him and arrive at a diagnosis, which he will later discuss, along with the suggestions for treatment, with his tutor. It was part of his pediatric training, and he was bent on cutting the mustard. For performing well on this task would definitely contribute to good notes on his report card.

In the elevator, he pushed the button indicating the children ward, which was just fifty yards from the elevator stop.

Once in the floor, he approached the nurse's station and crept up on a nurse who was busy making entries in a patient's chart.

"Hi, I am looking for the head nurse," was his question.

The busy nurse threw a short glance at him and pointed at a middle-aged woman in the center of the station, who was scouring for something in an open drawer of her desk.

He introduced himself once he was close to the nurse. "Hi, I am John Zangonini, a third-year medical student, and have a clinical assignment here." His right hand moved to his left breast pocket in search for his documents while talking to the nurse.

The head nurse continued the search in the drawer without glancing at him. "I was informed about it during the morning rounds." She lifted her head to look at the stranger in her ward. "Your assignment is in room 202." She continued her search.

John opened the door of room 202 slowly when there was no response to his three knocks and entered the room. Astonishment marked his face when his searching eyes located a little kid in bed, and no trace of a companion. Who was watching or entertaining the kid?

It crossed his mind that maybe the mother or other relatives vacated the room because they were notified of the pending visit of a medical student, and they left the room, making it easier for the student to finish his task. *It makes sense to me,* he thought, and kept investigating.

The room was shaped rectangularly. The northwest corner of it accommodated a child bed, its footboard toward south, where the entrance was. The headboard shared the wall on the north with a large picture window. Vertical railings about four inches apart boarded the side and the foot board of the bed, rendering it a safe place for the occupant.

The large window let enough light in the room, obviating the need to turn on the light until dusk. The oak tree visible through it was surrounded by many smaller trees, helping him to add to its majesty and justified its bragging. John, a tree lover all his life, was attracted by the view for a few seconds before his look was redirected to the little patient. He was kneeling behind the railings, his two puffy hands holding onto them, and his two large dark eyes fixed at him. John's love affair with the trees must have distracted him from his assignment, but the sight of the boy with his puffy hands holding on to the railing attracted him like a magnet and it took him few seconds to move his eyes towards his face.

The kid's eyes couldn't separate from him and were following his movements. John was focused on the boy's face. The bluish color of his swollen cheeks and lips looked permanent. The air entering his nostrils had to be forcefully pushed in to overcome the resistance inside.

John was trying to get hold of the reasons for the boy's hardship to breathe.

His huge stomach which was resting on his thighs grabbed his attention. That is why he was kneeling; it provided support to the large tumor in his stomach. The tumor's pressure on his abdominal vessels interfered with the circulation of blood; that was why the blood didn't get oxygenated well enough and made his lips and cheeks have a bluish appearance. He took two more steps towards the boy. The noise of pushing the air into his lungs was audible now, indicating to John the hardship the little boy had to overcome the increased pressure in his lungs due to the tumor.

John's eyes were anchored in the boy's body. He was stood there, frozen, like he had lost the sense of space. He wasn't braced for a little body to fight so much to overcome the hardships caused by a tumor, but it is something medical students learn in their training. Of course, the search for finding the reasons for his cancer had brought the memory of this little boy back to him and that he was comparing the cancer of a little boy with his own didn't cross his mind.

The fangs of grief kept him a prisoner for almost a minute before he could release himself and regain his composure.

John took another step and vanished the distance to the boy and introduced himself. "Hi, my name is John, and I am a third-year medical student." He couldn't continue.

The boy interrupted him, despite his breathing hardship. "What is a medical student?" was his question.

John responded, "A medical student is on his way to become a doctor like the ones treating you here, so you can go home and be with your mom again." John didn't wait for an answer. With his glance tossed at the boy's swollen hands, he continued, "What is your name?" Two large dark eyes stared at him. The bluish discolored lips moved while he was grasping for air. "My name is George."

"Oh, that is my favorite name, one of my best friend's name is George, too," he answered. A little smile occupied George's face.

John tossed a glance at George's swollen hands and continued. "How old are you?"

George was looking at him with his large eyes while struggling to overcome his breathing difficulties, and he needed few seconds to master his troubles. "I am four years old," he answered.

John not only had a hard time ignoring the little boy's difficulty to send air into his lungs, but it increased his longing for hugging him. He raised his arms around George and pressed him against his chest, not noticing the hard pressure of the railings against his arms. The warmth of George's body was soothing and penetrated John's body to its core. He could have kept the position for a long time, but after a minute of hugging, he slowly removed his arms. One could see in John's eyes how the mourning for the little boy had swallowed him when he asked, "Do you know why you are at this place and not at home with Mom?"

George looked at John's face as if he wanted to answer the question with his eyes and save his lips the struggle. A few seconds passed before a faint and fragile voice exited his mouth, "I have a big mass in my stomach," and he paused to grab some air. Apparently, the slightest activity consumed his entire energy. After few seconds, he broke his silence with the same fragile voice, "The doctors are going to remove it so my mom can take me home." The last word from him was a matter of guessing, since he was overwhelmed by the shortness of breath.

John stood in front of the bed, speechless. He wrapped his arms around him and, again, the soothing warmth emanating from George took him to another world. The knocking at the door had to be repeated a couple of times before he moved to the door and answered it.

The door opened slowly, and a nurse stood there. "His mother came to the station and insisted to be with her son again," she announced.

"She can return anytime she wishes," was John's answer.

When John was private with George again, he put his hand over his head and ran his fingers through his bushy hair, just looking at him.

He bent his head over George's head – his mouth touched

almost his ear – and he said under his breath, "It is time for me to leave. I will come back tomorrow, and we will have plenty to talk about." His love-filled eyes didn't distance from him. The door was opening slowly, and George's mother entered the room.

John whispered to George, "See you tomorrow," and left the room.

CHAPTER TEN

The next day, John was attending a pathology lecture. Its topic: children's mortality with cancer. It wasn't just part of his education in medicine; it had become personal since he had visited George.

George's tumor and the fate of the baby zebra were random acts of nature, he thought, and since the lecturer was using the word nature more than anything else, he felt justified to look at the George's tumor as one of the cruel actions of nature which had nothing to do with the personal experiences one had made in life.

The image of a little kid, his two puffy hands holding on to the railings of the bed and his large stomach resting on his thighs – the reason he was kneeling in the bed – had not quit John's mind. He was seeing him everywhere; even the seat beside him was occupied by George.

John followed his urge and left right after the lecture toward the pediatric ward of the university hospital. Yellowed and dried up leaves showed up all over the walkway from the lecture hall to the hospital. The bright sunshine made specks of brown in some of them visible. George entered the ward and walked toward room 202, his mind preoccupied with concocting a plan so George's mother would leave them alone during the interview.

He knocked at the door. There was no answer. He lifted his head and checked the number. It was correct. After his second knock remained unanswered, the idea that he might have been transferred entered his mind.

Pulling the door handle down made no noise, nor did opening the door slowly. His screening eyes astonished him immediately. They didn't detect any soul in the room.

Through the large window, the large oak tree was boasting its almost leafless branches, which attracted his attention for a little while.

After a few seconds, his glance averted to the floor. Its shining attested to its recent cleaning. The child bed in the corner revealed fresh sheets on the mattress and the pillow and the blanket. His glance lingered on the bed as if he was making sure George was really not present. Transfer of George to another room reentered his mind.

A short minute of walking took him to the nurse's station, and he approached two nurses. One nurse, who was pressing the receiver of the phone on her ear, very focused on her conversation, looked familiar to him. On closer glance, he recognized the head nurse whom he talked to yesterday.

With an abruptness and exhibiting no politeness, he interrupted the conversing nurse and brought up his question without introducing himself. The head nurse should remind him he saw her yesterday, was his thought.

"Room 202 is empty, where is the boy transferred to?" The agitation in his voice was obvious.

The nurse came a step closer to him and answered, "George is gone, he is with the angels now."

John's blank glance at her betrayed his lack of understanding the answer.

Looking upset and his voice raised, he responded, "What do you mean he is with the angels? He is my case assignment and I have come to finish my job."

The ferocity in his voice made the head nurse put down the receiver, its busy tone still ringing. She threw a scornful look at John and beckoned him to her desk. Once they were both seated, she asked John in a clear voice, "Anything I can do for you?" Her face was marked by disbelief that a third-year medical student couldn't fathom the meaning of 'he is with the angels'.

The head nurse was in her late fifties, slightly expanded outwards, with gray streaks in her black hair which she had parted on the left and neatly combed. She was almost as tall as John, who stood six feet.

John started his case without paying attention to the expression on her face.

"Well, I didn't finish my job yesterday; that is the reason for my return."

The nurse had difficulty to look at John with a clear face. She had a hard time expunging the expression of disbelief from her face. Apparently her mind couldn't provide her with an explanation for how a medical student didn't get the meaning of he was gone, regarding George.

Her doubtful eyes continued surveying John's face. After a short while, a voice with motherly tone vibrated the air. "George's terminal cancer was worsening by the hour. His lungs were filled with water. It was decided to transfer him to the ICU, but his mother didn't agree – 'The situation becomes more intolerable to see him depart this world with a lot of tubes attached to him. The ICU is not a magic place and the doctors in the ICU are not magicians,' she stated and continued, 'I have come to terms with the imminent departure of my son from this world, and the idea to prolong his life for couple of days doesn't have a place in my mind'. Obviously, without approval of his mother, a transfer was out of the question, and George stayed in the same room until the last minute."

At this point, her lips became motionless and her eyes were piercing John's face, as if she wanted to determine if John's mind had registered it.

A few seconds passed before she went on, "George's mother told me that her prayers were focused on the hope that when she meets him in another world, the reason for his early departure is brought to light."

Her eyes were directed at John when her voice, shadowed by a suggestion of sadness, continued her reporting. "George left us at ten thirty p.m. yesterday. I think his funeral is planned to take place in two days."

John stood there as if a bomb had exploded in front of him and the ensuing dust had concealed everything, including the nurse and John.

Almost a minute passed before he recovered and regained his composure. Heavy steps took him toward the exit. John didn't even recall if he had thanked the head nurse for the information.

The cold, bone-piercing wind, though refreshing, hit him when he stepped out. He eyed a bench under a mature linden tree with some of its yellow leaves scattered on the ground. An inviting place to rest and reflect on the events of the day. John perched on the bench. His behind was the conduit for the cold to transmit to his spine.

He put his elbows on his thighs and kept his head resting between the palms of his hands and tried to untangle his mind.

A medical student, a doctor in making, failed to finish his job because of emotional involvement. Was he fit to become a doctor? Was it an indicator that all his work was going up in smoke?

The questions gnawed at him. The desire for a warm place

moved him toward his dormitory, which wasn't far away.

Once in his room, he stretched on his twin bed positioned in the corner.

A desk was placed adjacent to it. It was small, so he could throw a glance through the medium sized window in front of it.

It took John few minutes to warm up while he stretched on the bed, looking up to the ceiling, his mind preoccupied with George's departure so much that the grumbling of his stomach went unnoticed.

He was trying to untangle his mind and find answers and he felt like somebody who is lost in a jungle without having a machete to clear his way.

If progressive cancer is so deadly, why does it occur in children? Is it to avoid the hardships while you are here? Is that the reason you depart? But all kids confront these hardships.

God threw his wrath on George at the innocent age of four, God the merciful? A deed more likely to be committed by the devil. But it must be a random act of nature, I have to conclude.

His search for an answer was lingering in his mind when, all of a sudden, Pete's image appeared in front of him.

CHAPTER ELEVEN

Pete, the tall and lanky guy, was a classmate in high school when he was a senior. Actually, he was the tallest of the class. His brownish hair rested on his long neck and always looked unkempt. A lock of his hair rested on his forehead permanently and was rolled back with the palm of his hand whenever he was engaged in a conversation with other classmates, a matter he wasn't aware of, but referring to him in his absence, simply rolling back the hair with the palm of the hand would make him present.

Pete looked through eyeglasses with fat black frames which rested on his prominent jawbones whenever he lowered his head to answer a classmate's question, usually regarding math or physics. His ability to solve problems in math or physics sometimes exceeded that of the teacher, leading to the belief among his classmates that someday he would be a shining star in physics or math.

The astonishment on the faces of the students listening to his announcement of being accepted into the school of divinity was infinite.

He added that he considered himself lucky to take part in the educational system and at the end call himself a theologian. The bewildered group of his fellow students dispersed after wishing him good luck.

There was one chair whose occupant didn't leave and was staring at him with questioning eyes. After a short moment, he stood up and walked with slow steps toward him. When he stood in front of him, the questions in John's eyes transferred to his lips.

"I am not here to quench my curiosity. I am genuinely interested why my dear friend who we thought was going to be a scientist will be a theologian".

Peter's answer came without any hesitation. "You know how pious my parents are, especially my mother, and it goes without a saying that my upbringing has been a religious one. I talk to God every day, I feel his presence everywhere and he leads all my deeds. He endowed me with the talent to absorb science easily."

At this point, Pete paused with his eyes directed to the ground, as if reflecting on something. After a short moment, he went on, "You know I revere privacy and sometimes I don't let a dear friend into what I call a private life."

He paused for few seconds while his eyes were screening John's face.

He continued, as if the expression on John's face had satisfied him.

"You have disclosed to me some aspects of your private life. Let me explain to you the experience which made me dedicate my life to the service of God." He went on, "It happened when I was eight. I had descended the school bus and was on my way to the kitchen when a puzzling surprise took hold of me. Instead of my mother, my father greeted me with a cup of coffee in his hand. His answer to my question of 'Where is Mom?' was to wrap his arm around my shoulder and press me against himself. A sense of a bad omen crept inside me. 'Is Mommy OK?' I asked with a fragile voice. My father tightened his grip and, with a voice hardly concealing his sadness, said, 'I came home earlier than usual because of your mother's call. She called me to be home with her because she wasn't feeling well and had fever. I took her right away to the hospital and they admitted her. I was waiting to go with you to visit her.'

"I was lost in the maze of my thoughts when I sunk in the back seat of the car. Are they going to cure her? Is she going to be back home soon? Sinking deeper in the seat was my reaction to find some calmness. My mind was being battered with questions like: *hospitals are places for sick people, some of whom miss returning home.* The thought increased the wetness in my eyes and shortly thereafter, I felt the tear drops on my face.

"My father, who was watching me through the mirror, slid his right arm through the front seats and I felt the gentle pressure of his right hand on my thigh and the words, 'Don't worry, she will be back home soon, I promise' His utterance had the effect of a sedative on me.

"The receptionist sitting behind the counter at the hospital was a middle-aged woman with salt and pepper hair, a double chin, and broad shoulders. Her smile was disarming.

"She was searching the room number of my mother. That is when her smile vanished and her face was occupied by more serious expression. 'Sorry you can't visit her now. She has been transferred to isolation unit. I am going to talk to the nurse in charge and if she finds the time, she will come down and report about your mother's condition.' She wanted to emphasize some of her words and went on, 'Of course the nurse will be down here when she is free.'

"About four to five minutes passed. A nurse appeared in the waiting area and was pointed to us by the receptionist.

'Hi, I am Shirly, working in the isolation unit.' And her head turned toward me when she continued, 'I understand you are here to see your mom.' I was holding my father's hand and looking at the empty chair, trying to avoid eye contact with her, and she continued without waiting for my response. 'Don't worry, you can hug your mom soon, but right now it is not possible.' She turned toward my father and went on, 'Your wife has sepsis, which we think is caused by a very contagious microbe. By tomorrow, we should have the microbiology result which will help us to decide to keep her in isolation or transfer her to a regular ward. At this point, multiple antibiotics are attacking the microbe and we are monitoring her circulatory and respiratory functions continuously.'

"My father thanked the nurse for the information and asked what was the appropriate time to return. 'Well, why don't you call tomorrow morning,' was her response.

"We walked toward the exit, hand in hand. At home, we sat on the couch. My father's look was empty and directed to the ground and I almost broke down to tears. That is when I felt the weight of my father's hand on my shoulder and he whispered into my ear, 'Mom is in God's hands. He will take good care of her.' The words were so calming that I put my head on his shoulder and closed my eyes.

"The moonshine was tossed on my bed and the carpet when my father tucked me in, pressed his lips against my cheek and wished me a good night.

"The room, illuminated by moonlight, reminded me of a flick I had watched a couple of weeks ago. The image of the man in prostrate position in a moonlit room, his arms and legs spread wide like he was in an eagle position, asking God for forgiveness, reappeared in front of me. Reappeared in front of me.

"I got out of bed and stretched on the carpet and assumed the same position and whispered, 'God, Dad told me Mom was in your hands. I know you are almighty, you took my beloved Rachel, I was told it was your will and there was always a purpose to it. Right now, I am sensing your presence and want to beg you, don't take my mom and I will dedicate my life to you spreading the news of your mercy.

"That night, I had a dream. Mom and I were returning from grocery store with full bags. Mom was refurbishing the fridge. A big smile occurred on her face when she told me, 'Well, you mentioned to me how hungry you were when I was confined to the hospital' and continued filling up the fridge.

"Mom retuned home few days later, worn but cheerful as always. Resumption of her daily routine and activity would have been very much delayed if she had heeded Dad's advice for more rest.

"The professional opinion credited the multiple antibiotics, modern machines and her robust immune system for her quick recovery. Well, it was their opinion and couldn't replace the thought which had occupied my mind. It was God's mercy."

Pete stopped talking. His eyes were probing John's face, as if he was questioning himself if John was a suitable person to whom he had revealed so much of his spirit, although he considered John a very close friend.

John was looking for spiritual help as far as George was concerned. The metamorphosis of Pete the science guy to Pete the spiritual guy made him the suitable person to look for, but where could he find him?

John recalled that most of his incidental encounters with Pete were at lunch time in cafeteria. A look at his watch confirmed that it was lunch time, and the cafeteria wasn't far from his dormitory.

A few minutes later, he was walking toward the cafeteria. He was about to enter it when he came across Pete. A coincidence? He thought it was God-sent.

"Hi, Pete, nice to see you. We haven't talked for ages."

A face full of surprise turned to him and smiled. "Don't exaggerate; we talked few days ago with each other."

"It appears to me like ages," John responded, and they entered the cafeteria.

While they were screening the area for an empty table, John pointed to him a table just being vacated. Pete chuckled and said, "You must have eagle eyes."

They approached it, tucked the chairs and put their derriere on the seats.

"What are you going to drink?" Pete asked.

John responded after tossing a glance at the table. "Actually, the drink is not what I am here for. I wanted to meet you because I thought you would have the answer to my question which has been gnawing at me. My orange juice can wait for me."

Pete's eyes pierced John's face for a moment before he moved his lips. "Why don't you go ahead with what is troubling your mind," not being aware of a lock of hair covering his forehead. His eyes, from behind the black framed glasses, continued piercing John's face.

John responded without hesitating. "I always appreciated how you tackled a problem." He paused for an instant and tossed a glance at Pete. "I don't mean a math or physics problem. My trouble is how one is relating to other human beings."

A serious expression appeared on Pete's face before John continued. "I will be brief and get right to the point. Part of my medical training requires working up a patient who will be chosen by a tutor. My assignment was a little boy with terminal cancer." John paused. At this point, he had to clear his throat. "The boy had to break his sentences or keep them short because of shortness of breath. His hands, his face, actually, his entire body was puffed up due to water accumulation.

"He couldn't stand on his feet and had to kneel in order to use his thighs as a resting place for his huge abdomen, which was the location of his big tumor. I don't know if the tumor was that big or part of protruding of the abdomen was due to water accumulation."

John paused, staring into space. He needed the respite to regain his composure and few seconds passed before he could continue. "The condition of the boy totally devastated me, so that my intention about writing a summary of my case and present it to my clinical tutor evaporated. My emotional involvement was so overwhelming that instead of examining him, I hugged him, and since then my mind hasn't ceased to ask why little kids are chosen to endure so much.

"The next day, I returned and was determined to finish my job, but I was told the boy had departed the earth."

John's eyes were staring into the space, and he was silent. Pete honored it and didn't try to break it; he was just staring at John.

John continued after a while, "Since his departure, a sense of depression has taken hold of me and the question returns to my mind again and again: 'why does a kid have to leave before having experienced the joys and sufferings of life?'"

John's eyes were fixed at the table, as if he was looking for an answer there, or was he looking for George? A gentle squeeze by Pete brought him back. Pete was looking at him with compassion and his voice was very calming when he started talking. "I feel very sorry for the boy, my heart goes to his mourning and suffering parents. May God give them the strength to deal with this tragedy."

A flabbergasted John threw a look of puzzlement and disbelief at Pete. His mind was looking for an answer to the question why a little boy had to depart this world before being exposed to its joys and sorrows; instead, Pete delivers something which sounds like a priest's sermon.

Pete wasn't disturbed by John's look at his face and went on with the same comforting voice, "Your compassion shows that you are equipped with the qualities to deal with human suffering. Your first patient encounter was a little boy who didn't experience all beauties of life and also didn't face its sufferings; he left us while still innocent."

Pete stopped talking and was staring into space. Actually, he was trying to break the resistance inside himself about talking of departure of his beloved Rachel.

After a silence which lasted almost a minute, he turned his head toward John. His look betrayed that he had overwhelmed the inner resistance and was ready to dig up the memory he had buried deep inside.

He went on, with his voice on the lower side, "Let me answer your question with my story of loss which devastated me when I was seven years old. My aunt and her husband were the happy parents of Rachel and her two younger siblings. They lived just two houses away from me. Rachel was my age, and we visited the same school. Actually, we shared the same classroom and walked home together; the school wasn't far away from our homes. Most evenings we spent together either in her or my house.

"I was so fond of her that one day, at the kitchen table, I told my mom when I grew up I would marry her. She chuckled and said OK while running her fingers through my hair." Pete stopped at this point and smiled at John.

The smile gradually diminished in size and vanished. It was replaced in his face with lines of sadness when he continued.

"The day she was absent in classroom, I felt part of me was missing, though it had never occurred to me that she was part of me.

"The first sentence coming out of my mouth when I got back home was, 'Why was Rachel absent from school today?'

"My mother looked at me with a face heavy with concern and worry and said, 'She didn't feel well and had fever. We had to take her to the hospital, and they told us they had to work her up and probably she would stay there for few days.' My glance at my mother was silent, though a turmoil started ravaging my head. After a while, I told my mother I had to finish some homework and headed toward my room, the room I spent countless hours with Rachel in and sometimes had to listen to the call from downstairs to be quiet.

"I laid in bed, contemplating about Rachel, searching for a way to cope with my time without her the next few days. After an hour of pondering, I made my way downstairs and was on time in the kitchen for dinner. The food on the table didn't attract me. The bite I took made me retch so badly that it raised the hope in my mind that my mother would take me to the hospital, where I could spend the night where Rachel was. My mother connected the dots and arrived at the root of the problem.

"In a calm voice she announced that I didn't have to grab any food if it made me sick. After a minute of viewing my eyes, which were fixed at the food without my hand making any move for it, she took me upstairs to my room and tucked me in. The warmth of her breath when she pressed her lips against my cheek was very comforting and her whisper into my ear that a good sleep can perform miracles took me shortly thereafter to the slumber dominion.

"I don't recall if it was in my dreams, or if I had overheard my mother talking to my dad about an article she had read about reactive depression. It didn't require a genius to find out to whom it alluded to.

"For a week, I was like a cat sitting on hot bricks and I asked my mom multiple times when Rachel was coming back, but her answer was always evasive. Last time I asked, she responded that she wasn't sure, maybe tomorrow. In retrospect, her answer was her desperate way to avoid the real situation. The next day when school was over, I didn't walk fast home, I was running home with the hope to meet Rachel.

"Once at home, I saw my mom. Without looking at her, my question waiting for her jumped out of my mouth. 'Is Rachel back home?'

"She was sitting on the corner of the couch and turned her head slowly toward me. When I saw her red eyes and her grief-stricken face, the premonition of a disaster possessed me all over. Her red eyes, betraying countless drops of tears, nevertheless glimmered when she looked at me.

"She extended her arms and grabbed me, set my behind on her thighs and started squeezing me against her chest. When she put her cheek on my face and I felt the wetness on her skin, I knew something terrible had happened. A minute passed without her mouth opening and she had to release her right arm to wipe her face. Then she looked at me with her wet eyes and said under her breath, 'Rachel passed away'

"I didn't fully understand her and was looking at her with a puzzled face.

"She explained with the same voice, 'Passed away means she is no more with us in this world.'

My heart dropped, the air became thick with gloom and I think I was filling my face with ignorance as a last ray of hope that she wasn't dead. I asked directly, 'Is Rachel dead?'

'Yes, she died eight hours ago,' she responded and went on, 'They told me she was inflicted with a progressive form of leukemia which made her body powerless to face any infection and she succumbed to it'

"I still was lost in the definition. Dying applied to old people, to grandmas and grandpas, but Rachel was only seven years old; it was like an insolvable puzzle or something incomprehensible to me.

"I pressed my head against my mother's chest and tried to show my lack of understanding. 'But Rachel was only a kid'

"She kissed my head, lifted me and set me on the chair across from the couch and took some paper to wipe her eyes, threw a glance at me and said, "When God needs angels, he picks up kids from the earth. Rachel is an angel now, an angel in the divine world. When we get there when our times has come, we will meet her again.'"

Pete was silent for a moment, then he squarely looked into John's eyes and said, "I believed her every word. They have kept me on even keel since."

Pete was quietly staring into the space. His eyes averted to John. "Well, you were asking me about George, the little boy who departed this world. I described Rachel's departure, which I am glad I did. I couldn't have expected a better occasion or a closer friend for bringing it up from the deep corner of my soul where I had buried it."

He was silent and was enjoying the relief, the recounting of the events had provided. After a few seconds, he fixed his eyes at John's and said, "You know that I still believe in my mom's explanation?"

The encounter with Pete had made a deep impression on his mind. Pete's explanation, which he had embraced from his mom, sounded weird to John. On the other hand, he thought Pete was going to be a priest; priests serve god and the angels he created and Pete's answer naturally will involve angels.

It was hard to fall asleep when your mind is being bombarded with such considerations. The next day, he had an appointment with his tutor and, of course, a refreshed student is in better form to explain his failure not to finish his clinical assignment.

His bewildering thoughts were gnawing on his mind until the darkness pulled him and all his concerns inside his realm.

CHAPTER TWEVE

The sun had already lit up the room when his eyelids opened up and exposed him to the new day, the memory of Pete and George still fresh in his mind. His explanation of his failure regarding George to his tutor sounded to him as if he was speaking it today.

He was bent on continuing his treatment, no matter if the search of his thoughts and memories brought him closer to finding a cause for his cancer, for today was his appointment with Dr. Levinson the oncologist.

After the breakfast he was seen at Levinson's and the same treatment with the same nurse was repeated followed by radiation.

He got quite curious when he returned home. The smell of food dominated the air. He thought Jane was preparing something in the kitchen.

The absence of Jane was the cause of his disappointment. The thought that she must have used her lunch break to prepare something for him hit his mind and a look at the counter confirmed his guess.

A broiled sea bass with basmati rice and a variety of vegetables in a large white plate placed on the kitchen counter was still faintly warm.

John's taste buds got excited and after, taking it out of microwave, they got content to come in touch with it.

Meanwhile, weeks passed. A tired John was on his way home after chemo. At home, he pushed Mozart's requiem into the CD player, stretched on the couch and was immersed deeper and deeper in the sound until he was part of it. It was his way to overcome the nausea of chemo. Indeed, he was so lost in the music that his auditory hardly registered the noise the ringing bell was producing. A while passed before he became aware of it. He got up and walked toward the entrance.

A total surprise overwhelmed him when he saw Don and not the mailman as expected.

Don, his dear colleague with whom he was so often in cafeteria at lunchtime. He gleamed and the corners of his lips went upward. Don was about to mention something when he was interrupted by John. "It renders me speechless to see you standing in front of my house, the mere joy it injects into me is indescribable." He extended his arms and hugged Don tightly while saying, "Let's get in and have some coffee".

In the living room, before even taking a seat, John had to convey his happiness to Don's presence. "I am not just seeing you, you have brought the whole department with you; it makes me feel I have restarted working." He wrapped his arms around his shoulder and hugged him again.

"I wish the circumstances were more propitious, like the time we were having lunch in the Mexican restaurant," Don responded while his left hand moved toward his right breast pocket and pulled out an envelope and said, "This is for you. You mentioned a few seconds ago that my presence to you represented the whole department, and I must agree that the whole department wants you back as soon as possible, and I have brought it to you with the envelope."

John's hand was scouring in the drawer for an envelope

opener while Don's eyes moved to his watch and, after a glimpse, he said, "I am sorry, I have to leave. My case is scheduled in thirty minutes".

He gave John a quick hug and said, "I will see you later. Get well soon," and left.

John was sitting on the couch, his eyes fixed at the envelope, which he had placed on the coffee table. It made him feel to be with his other colleagues in the department meeting. His extreme fatigue, something he had to live with in the last two months of chemotherapy, in addition to nausea, overburdened him. His eyelids slid down without him putting up any resistance and soon he was in the lap of Morpheus.

When he woke up, a glimpse at his watch disclosed his eyes were fallen to darkness for almost thirty minutes.

He was screening the room for something. That is when Don's presence and the envelope he brought with crossed his mind. He threw a look toward the coffee table and grabbed the envelope and ripped it open.

There was a card inside, which he pulled out. His look for a letter was in vain. The front of the card showed the picture of a garden with tall trees and rows of dense roses, daffodils, and hibiscus, which the silvery sunshine breaking through the branches of the tall trees made more colorful.

He unfolded the card. All the staff members were wishing him a quick recovery. He was reading the names: Jack Cooperman, Johnny Rodrigues, Shirly Smith, Don Wilson, and he stopped. Don was there and brought the card, but that wasn't the reason he stopped. Don reminded him of his good old days, when his salivary glands were not destroyed by the radiation.

Don had introduced him to quesadillas of his life, long before he was robbed of his saliva. He tossed another glimpse at the card and thanked Don Wilson to have offered him the opportunity before the daemon had taken up residence in his throat.

The imagination of Don at his side as they were heading toward the Mexican restaurant, with Don carrying a big bottle of water to help him overcome the dryness in his mouth whenever he needed it, just added to his grief.

But it wasn't long time ago he was in cafeteria having lunch with Don when he mentioned quesadillas. "You have to try it at this restaurant, it will stay in your memory as one of the best quesadillas you have ever tasted."

The meeting of the department was over and each attending was on his way to make rounds, except Don, who walked toward John and mentioned to him, "Don't forget, today we will eat at the Mexican restaurant and you will have the unique experience of your life to taste the best quesadilla in the world." A chuckle followed before he went on, "I will meet you there at twelve noon," and walked out.

John's mind was still preoccupied with the lack of saliva in his mouth.

It took him almost an hour to persuade himself that the Mexican restaurant was a thing of the past when he was as fit as a fiddle, but right now he had to deal with the aftermath of radiation, but it goes without saying that the experience in the restaurant had etched itself into his mind powerfully. It was almost noon, and he was sitting in the car, driving west toward the restaurant. The sun visor was not a match for the heavy sunshine, and he had to readjust it many times, although he had sun glasses on.

After ten minutes, a nondescript building as the site of the restaurant, which John could have passed easily, matched his address.

The large capital letters on its front glass door announced ELBEER.

The menu was attached to the right side of the entrance and had to compete with a copper lantern showing a green patina.

Inside, the square tables with marble tops were arranged randomly, which was a good way to distract from the smallness of dining hall.

John was screening the tables when a waiter approached and rushed him to the table Don had reserved and was waving at him from, tucked the chair and offered it with the palm of his hand to John.

The naïve Mexican paintings on the wall gave the restaurant a Mexican flair, though the smell of Mexican food wafting in the air couldn't distract your mind of being in a Mexican restaurant.

John was sipping his Corona when the waiter returned and placed two plates on the table.

"Bon appetit," he said and left. On each plate, a flour tortilla was rolled so completely as to conceal the content, though the melted cheese was almost flowing out, an indication of delicious things it was covering.

When John bit into his quesadilla, his taste buds betrayed to him the inside filling of the quesadillas: baby spinach sprinkled with blue cheese and sautéed onion, and some special spices hugged pieces of sautéed chicken with herbs he couldn't name, all soaked in melted asiago cheese.

John's first bite had pleased him so well that he turned toward Don and said, "You are right, it tastes heavenly,"

The memorable impression of the quesadilla on John was so deep that whenever they met, John asked Don, "When are we going to that restaurant again?"

Now, though Don had left, the memory became so vivid that it created the sensation of wetness in his mouth. His finger checked his tongue and reminded him of the havoc radiation had produced in his mouth.

Although he was about to call Don to reserve a table at the Mexican restaurant, he was quick to scratch the idea. In reality, the memory of the food was bringing back the wetness in his mouth, but was it really his mouth or just the memory? He was very much aware of the destruction caused by radiotherapy.

CHAPTER THIRTEEN

Jane's professional life started at Lions Gate high school. Since her childhood, the idea to become a teacher had taken a firm spot in her mind, and she had started to dream of young souls who discussed a literary subject with her and sometimes even challenged her views. Since she majored in English literature, not a day passed without her being lost in the depth of a book or engaged her friends or guests in literary discussion.

Her acceptance at Lions Gate as the English teacher had fascinated her. The fact that starting at seven thirty a.m. meant to get up before the sun does didn't bother her. Though one aspect of the classroom, as she found out later, constituted the ugly part of her job. The class was stained, with students who were not eager to participate in the process of learning. Some called these specks difficult students, for others they were just troublemakers. That their brains were not at the level of others they were disturbing, nobody dared to mention. And no matter how much time she spent with them, no matter, she never abandoned them, though the futility of her efforts was obvious to her.

At the end of the day, her savior was her inborn trait of patience, which was one of the contributors to help her establish her reputation among the staff and the students as helpful and calm.

Her colleagues were used to her smile whenever they passed by her, and their numbers who sought her advice for their personal problems grew by the day and at lunch time her table looked busy by few more chairs tucked in from other places. She cherished her status among her students and colleagues and was very thankful for the life she was blessed with.

The day John announced to her that his body was invaded by a daemon who was at work to insidiously destroy it, changed the picture. Her outstanding patience with the students, her exemplary interactions with her colleagues became a thing of the past. The smiling face with which she encountered the questions of students changed into a lugubrious and sometimes just a grim face. More students were ordered out of classroom just for trivial reasons than ever.

One day in cafeteria, a colleague sitting across from her spilled her coffee. The brown liquid flew across the vinyl-topped table and reached her plate. She suddenly leapt out of her place disgustfully and uttered in a raised and irritated voice, "Can't you be more careful?" The disbelief it created in the glances of her colleagues was undeniable.

Very soon, a rumor circulated among the staff that Jane had a marital problem, serious enough to affect her behavior at the school.

Many thought a problem which makes you change your attributes of helpfulness, calmness and friendliness is serious enough to bring it to the attention of principal.

The chair Jane was perched on faced to Judy, the principal. Judy looked much younger than her actual age; she was appointed principal at the age of forty-five, three years earlier. She was the youngest principal in the district. Her black hair was parted in the middle and reached the nape of her neck; her small nose, thin lips and smooth skin were the reasons some waiters had to look at her twice when she ordered wine.

At her desk, sitting opposite to Jane, her eyes were glancing at Jane as if pleading with her, "Please help me to come to term with this difficult situation, I am just trying to help you." Her look at Jane continued for few seconds before she started talking. "Let me emphasize, I am aware of your behavioral changes. In the past two months, whenever we cross paths, a fleeting "hi" jumps out of your mouth and you hurry up passing me, as if you were in a rush. The sweet smile on your face which brought joy to me has vanished. We used to be regular guests at each other's house, enjoying the company of our friends."

Judy stopped at this point as if expecting a response, but Jane was silent and continued her glance at Judy.

Judy went on after few seconds, "You know well this is not the reason we are sitting here face to face. The reason is the rumor spreading among your colleagues about you. I am glad this meeting is not because a complaint was made about you and—" Judy stopped talking and was looking straight into Jane's eyes as if expecting a response. Since Jane didn't break her silence, she continued. "We are friends, good friends who help each other. What is the reason you are behaving in a different way? You can have confidence in me, nobody will get wind of what you tell me. Is it a marital problem?"

Judy paused while staring at her and extended her right arm and grabbed Jane's left hand, which rested on the desk, and squeezed it gently. While her glance was fixed at her, she continued in a low voice, "Of course, I am asking you to spill the beans, but I reassure you that I respect your privacy." She stopped and for a second pierced into Jane's eyes, as if her next question was going to be a direct one. She went ahead and asked promptly, "Is it John?"

"It is not John, and we don't have marital problems," came

out of the mouth of Jane while she was staring at the desktop.

When she straightened up her head, two welled-up eyes were looking at her. Her lips moved slowly, and a fragile voice uttered, "I have to correct myself. It is John. He was diagnosed with advanced cancer two months ago and currently is undergoing treatment". She had to lower her head toward the desk and wipe the wet stains on it with her right hand.

Judy was silent. Her silence couldn't conceal the expression of shock on her face. After a few seconds, she stood up and approached Jane with slow steps. She wrapped her arms around Jane's shoulder and they hugged.

Judy's cheek pressing against Jane's emanated a warmth which penetrated gradually into Jane's inside and eased her tension. When they unhugged, Jane kept her face close to hers, as if she didn't want to miss feeling the warm air coming out of her nose.

Jane's eyes threw an apologetic glance at Judy and she said, "I am sorry, I should have informed you much earlier."

Jane was on her way home and an idea dominated her thoughts.

To take John for a walk would be so relaxing. Passing by the tall trees, bushes and dried up lawns will help her bring down her tensions.

Maybe during the time of walking she could bring up her meeting with Judy. Persuading John to go with her was the major problem to overcome, judging by her previous attempts to get him outside for a walk.

He never got tired repeating his old excuses: "I don't want to tumble across an acquaintance in my condition," or, "What if I meet a patient unexpectedly, how am I going to explain to her my terrible shape?"

He always succeeded in staying home and listening to his favorite music and depriving her from fresh air, her metaphor for a walk.

In her search for a way to get John out of the house, finally she concocted a plan. She knew John would never reject anything based on her desire, so her sentence would start with: *I haven't gone for a walk with you hand in hand in the neighborhood for ages, you think you are able to do it for me?* She started feeling her skin prickling, just to walk around with John.

A silent house greeted her. She went right away to the stairway. John was either sleeping or just resting, the quiet of the house betrayed to her. A nap after finishing his radiotherapy was almost a routine.

She approached the bedroom discretely. The bedroom door was a crack open, through which Brahms piano concerto vibrated. Although it was very soft, her auditory system registered it.

She opened the door and stretched herself beside John without expressing a word; the enjoyment of sharing the moment with John and listening to the score was tremendous.

The wall behind the short headboard revealed a lot of pictures nailed to it. It was the image of Josh, their son, who took her twenty years back, when she first met John, and three years later, Josh was born. The mesmerizing moment didn't let her notice she was running her fingers through John's hair. She uttered under her breath, "Please don't leave me," and extended her left arm around him, laid her cheek on John's forehead and together they were lost in the piano concerto. Her concocted plan for a walk was relegated to the future.

CHAPTER FOURTEEN

November arrived. John was on the way to his car from Dr. Levinson's office. He had a long discussion with him about continuing his treatment. The results of today's visit were not encouraging.

The questions of carrying on the therapy or just quit it and let the disease take its course had preoccupied his mind for a couple of weeks. The support he was looking for was not provided by his oncologist. The bottle he was carrying in his hand betrayed how he was supporting his dry mouth. The radiation was too successful in destroying his salivary glands, and he was bent on assisting the little army left in his tongue and cheek, who fought tooth and nail to maintain the rest of his salivary production.

The chemotherapy was, of course, responsible for his shrinking; his coat felt loose, as if he was showing off by wearing his older brother's coat.

Dr. Levinson's answer, "Don't give up on chemo or radiation, you have no say in this matter, these are the only options you have," didn't cool off the heated debate in his mind if he should go ahead and quit the therapy. John's glance at him must have conveyed to him his disbelief, for Levinson added to his statement, "Give your body's defense a respite, it will be more ready afterwards."

John's look wasn't convincing when he left Levinson's office.

The way to his car was half through and the bone touching cold was a reminder of the winter ahead. The bright sunshine on his face was pleasing but couldn't ease the bone chilling cold.

Back at home, the first thing he did was to load his CD-player with Schubert's eight and lie on a couch listening to it. His eyes were fixed at the ceiling while he was trying to unwind. Schubert's unfinished symphony blasted through the air, but couldn't help him arrive at a decision not to finish the treatment. The fatigue was overwhelming him, and he closed his eyes to think over the consequences of stopping the treatment. That is when the darkness took over and he gave up resisting his eyelids' downward motion and said "hi" to his afternoon nap.

When he opened his eyes thirty minutes later, a deep sense of relaxation had possessed his body and the cloudless sky had kept the room bright.

He turned his head toward the window to see the ancient oak tree. He was looking for approval to quit his treatment anywhere and if the branches were hanging down, his beloved ancient friend agreed with him. In his desperation, anything supporting his decision was welcome. To him, looking at the tree was like looking at a painting.

The three feet diameter trunk was as sturdy as before, expanding with thick arms which branched in thinner ones and gave the tree a dense crown.

It surpassed the roof of the house but didn't touch it. Though the branches had lost most of their leaves, they were not hanging down. They revealed some welted leaves still holding on, a far cry from the luscious leaves in whose shadow he found refuge from sweltering heat, his hands holding on to the lawn mower. The ground was dotted with yellow leaves. The more he looked at the branches, the more he became aware of the ridiculousness of his thought of hanging branches. His look was fixed at the leaves kissing the ground. A few seconds passed before he lifted his head to look at the branches and the leaves still hanging and not starting their winter journey.

He caught himself counting them. It revitalized the memory of a story he had read many years ago, the story of the last leaf by a master storyteller, and he was the teenager reading the story.

The girl was bedridden with high temperature and was staring through the window at ivy branches. There were only few leaves left when she counted them. A fixed idea entered her mind: when the last one falls, she will die.

The next morning, she looked through the window; the last leaf was still hanging, and she recovered.

The last leaf was not a real one; it was painted on the wall by a painter who lived in the same building and had been waiting for the day when he creates his masterpiece, and he had succeeded. Though his recollection of a story he read many years ago was not complete, nevertheless he was caught in its net.

His eyes were staring at the oak tree branches and he started counting the leaves still hanging. There were thirty-two of them still hanging. While he was watching, one leaf couldn't resist the faint wind and joined the crunched ones on the ground.

He screened the other branches; there were many leaves which were dried up and still hanging. This eased his mind, for nobody would cross his mind who could paint the last leaf for him. The wishful thinking of a master who would create the painting made his lips assume the moon's first few days of shape. It was the sound of Jane's voice which terminated his fantasies.

"I am back home, are you ready?"

"Ready for what?" he responded. He was waiting for a response when suddenly yesterday's scene in in the kitchen unfolded in front of his eyes.

He had finished his high protein liquid – of course, with a lot of urging and pleading coming out of Jane's mouth – when Jane looked straight at his face and said, "I want to go out tomorrow evening."

"That is OK. I will probably be resting when you leave," he responded.

She grabbed his arm to emphasize what she was saying, "I want to go out with you, I said."

John's glance at her was a puzzled one when he responded, "Don't you recall my resentment for food? Last time I threw a glance at the spaghetti Bolognese, I almost threw up, though it is one of my favorite foods."

She grabbed his arm again. A thin layer of water covered her eyes when she answered, "I don't mean going out for dinner. The last three months, I haven't gone to a store with you and I miss it." Her voice was fragile when she stated that. Her voice vibrated with the same fragility once she continued, "I want to go shopping; promise you will accompany me?"

It was clear to John that he had no option but to give in to her demand; to hurt her feelings had never found a spot in his mind.

The voice announcing his response was resigned and low. "When are we leaving" he asked.

"As soon as I am back from work," was her response.

Meanwhile, the smell of freshly brewed coffee wafted through the air.

Caffeine still perked him up, and he wasn't sure if it was the culprit which made the scene escape from his memory or had he relegated it to his subconscious.

Though he resented to be seen in public in his declined

shape, the answer Jane's ears registered was, "In ten minutes."

The parking lot of the store was full. Jane checked the front rows one more time, that is when her eyes caught an empty spot and she occupied it right away. With leisurely steps they walked toward the entrance of the store. The occasional faint but cold blow of wind didn't make them adding speed to their steps. The wind won on intensity, the freezing cold hit their face, as if somebody was rubbing their face with ice cube. The prospect of warm air in the store forced them to move faster.

They entered the store. John was overwhelmed by the expanse of the store. The huge area was alive with many shoppers. The vents with their continuous flow of warm air did a good job in keeping the temperature at a comfortable level.

The aisles between the clothing racks were so narrow that made walking in double file almost impossible. Single or double file didn't make much of a difference, since the store was replete with shoppers, many in the aisles with some pieces of clothing in hand, headed toward the fitting room.

The vents were, of course, blowing warm air, but the moisture brought in by some shoppers and some wet folded umbrellas for good measure proved to be too much for the vents – in some areas, the rain must have been too heavy. The moisture in the air was negligible as far as the shoppers were concerned, but John's lungs were quick to convey to him the feeling of heaviness.

Jane was busy scouring a blouse rack. One grabbed her attention and she stretched it between her two hands and asked John, "So, what do you think? You like it?"

John's glance at the blouse was charged with disinterest and he uttered, "It looks nice."

Jane replaced it with a face hardly capable of hiding her disappointment.

John felt the heaviness in his lungs was getting worse while he was struggling through the aisles. He turned his head toward Jane and asked, "Is this place always so crowded?"

"Yes, hon, it is an outlet store," was her quick response.

John looked at her with impatience and asked, "How long are we going to be here"

"Hon, I am looking for a blouse and jeans, as soon as I have found acceptable ones we will be out of here," she responded swiftly.

John turned his face to her and said, "I need some fresh air." He placed a kiss on her cheek and went on, "I will be waiting for you at the entrance." Slow steps took him toward the exit without waiting for an answer,

The chill which was penetrating John's face was invigorating and refreshed his mind. His eyes screened the outside area. The store was shaped rectangularly: its long side faced the parking lot, a pedestrian walkway led along its length to the next street. He started walking slowly to the next street. The large windows alongside the length of the store allowed a look inside. John tried to locate Jane and wave at her. The number of racks bursting with different clothing was mindboggling; the numerous shoppers on the aisles scouring the racks or checking the price tags made looking for Jane like looking for the needle in the hay sack.

He turned his head toward the end of the store. A narrow street separated it from the stores located on next area.

The shops on the other side were smaller and well-illuminated.

He crossed the narrow street to have a look of other shops.

The first one on the corner attracted him like a magnet. It was a pet store. No wonder about its magical power on him; his love for animals was inborn and was nourished when his parents presented him with a St. Bernard puppy when he was four years old. By the time he had reached age six, he was allowed to walk the dog without an accompanying adult.

The proud memory of some adult passersby stopped to pet his big puppy and sometimes asking what his name was had occupied a firm niche in his soul. He still recalled the proudness in his voice when he was giving some information about his big puppy to an adult.

He peeped into the store. The different animals kept in cages brought a smile to his face, a testimony of his desire to do his heart good and explore the store.

Once in the store, the voice of a middle-aged woman made him to turn his head toward the cage. The woman was standing in front of it and trying to make the green feathered bird to imitate her voice. She was repeating, "Say pumpkin," again and again, to no avail. John's eye met a face thick with frustration.

Hardly a minute later, a husky voice averted his glance toward a man standing behind him. "What can I do for you?"

John responded, "Thank you, I am just browsing."

"Let me know if anything interests you," answered the man with husky voice.

"Surely I will," John responded. His glance was following him returning to his desk. The way he had approached John, or was it something in his voice that prompted John to think he wasn't just the salesman but also the owner?

Meanwhile, John started screening the cages left to the middle-aged woman, which showed birds of many kinds looking in different directions. His eyes moved farther to the left cages with puppy dogs as their occupants. Just across from the desk of the salesman, who was busy giving some advice on the phone, his eyes caught the sight of a bigger cage. It was wooden. Bars four inches apart comprised its front and a puppy was looking at him through its bars.

John approached the cage while his eyes never stopped staring at him.

He stood in front of the cage. The puppy was relatively large; the fell on his head was in touch with the roof of the cage. His face was pushing through the front bars, as if he was trying to get out and jump into John's chest.

The two large dark eyes had engrossed John. The longer he kept staring at them, the lighter he felt. At some point, he felt so light that he started floating and fell into the room where George was accommodated and was looking through the wooden bars of his bed at him. The sadness flowing out of his eyes was so overwhelming that he approached him to touch his head when a husky voice brought him back to the real world. "It looks like you are interested in this puppy."

John's ears were deaf to the steps of the salesman. His voice was like a bolt from the blue. His surprised face turned to the salesman.

The salesman's eyes were looking at him and he continued, "Let me tell you the story of this puppy." He chuckled as if he was he was about to start a funny tale. He went on, "We didn't buy him nor was he brought in by someone looking for a shelter for him."

John was quick to ask, "Then how did he get here?"

"Well, that is very interesting," were the words of the salesman. "When we came in this morning, he was sitting at the entrance, looking at me. I lifted him up and didn't encounter any resistance, as if he wanted to be taken in." He paused for a little while, then a big smile flashed on his face, and he went on, "Today is our vet day; the veterinarian has come and vaccinated all new arrivals if they needed it."

He looked at John's face, as if studying the effects of his statements, and went on, "He is an Akita puppy. They have a well behavior. You want to take it?"

John tossed a glance at the puppy and asked, "How old is he?"

"Well, judging by his size, I would say eight to ten months," uttered the salesman.

John's look averted to the cage. A joyful smile took shape on his face and he said, "I will take him."

He paid the price, got the vaccination document and, with the puppy resting on his chest, walked out of the store.

As soon as he was outside, he lifted the puppy and put his cheek on his head. The faint blow of the cold wind was enough to prickle the puppy's fur against John's skin, who felt not only the warmth but a new energy in his body.

John started with slow steps, walking toward the store to meet Jane, holding the puppy firmly in his chest. The cold air, a harbinger of the soon coming winter, was refreshing, though he wasn't registering the cold in his lungs. His olfactory sense was touched by the smell of roses. For a while, he thought he was walking in a rose garden. His time in the garden was cut short by a familiar sound. He turned his head and saw Jane, whose voice was becoming louder.

"John don't go any farther. I am standing here by the entrance." John reversed his steps toward the entrance of the store, where Jane was standing with a shopping bag in her hand.

"Where are you going? I have been waiting for you here for

ten minutes," but stopped suddenly, her baffled eyes fixed at the dog John was holding in his chest. It took her few seconds to separate her eyes from the dog and ask John, "What the hell is that dog doing on your chest?"

Jane was aware of John's fondness for dogs, but waiting for him for ten minutes in the cold and seeing him passing by, then discovering he was holding a puppy in his chest, struck her like a thunder.

John was careful not to aggravate Jane's shock and responded in a calm voice, "I was in a pet store where I saw him; it was love at first sight and I bought him." His glowing eyes changed directions and tossed a glance at him, and he pressed his newly found trophy tighter to his breast. His face glittered, a rarity in the last three months, and they headed toward the car.

John's joyful face had a calming effect on Jane and helped her to break out of her agitated mood. She looked at John and, with a tone in her voice trying to sound as normal as it could be, asked, "What are you going to call him?"

"His name is George," he responded quickly. She extended her right arm to envelop his neck and pressed her lips on John's head before pressing the gas pedal.

Once at home, she couldn't resist the urge to check her shopping bag.

She grabbed it and pulled a pair of dark gray jeans out. Her hands holding the upper part, she spread it in the air and asked John, who was engaged with George, "What do you think? Isn't it adorable?"

John turned toward Jane. His questioning eyes were asking, "Did you ask me anything?"

Jane, already annoyed by John's attention to George, responded with a loud voice, "Yes, I was addressing you. Do you like my new jeans?"

John answered with indifference, "Yes, they look nice."

Her face dropped as she realized John's lack of interest and involvement in her new acquisition. John's fondness for dogs was known to her, but that one day a puppy will dominate his interest had never dawned on her. He was so engrossed with him that she left him alone and headed toward the kitchen and said, "I am was going to prepare dinner. Are you hungry?"

What a question, she thought on her way. Lately, she had the feeling as if she was force feeding him. John was preoccupied with George; that is when his ears acted as being deaf to Jane's voice. She glanced few more seconds at John; at once, she realized the only way to distract him from George was by yelling.

John kept his arms wrapped around George. That way he kept feeling the new energy which was entering his body. The new vigor was so uplifting he felt he was floating in the air. At one time, he saw a garden with waterfalls and a cornucopia of lush green hills, an abundance of variegated flowers and bushes, and he was walking with George there.

Jane returned from the kitchen to announce that dinner was ready, but she had to stop and stare at John and George.

John's arms were wrapped around George tightly, his eyes staring into space as if they were experiencing another world. Her look at them continued for a while before she made her statement that dinner was ready and had to repeat it with a louder voice, since John didn't show any reaction to her first statement.

The loud voice had grabbed the attention of John, whose questioning eyes diverted toward her and made her repeat her statement, "I said dinner was ready."

"Did you make anything for George," John asked.

"Yes, I did," was her response.

The smell of sautéed vegetable and tomato sauce and salmon drifted in the kitchen. John, with George comfortably resting in his chest, followed the scent coming from the kitchen.

The sight of a steaming bratwurst set on a plate on the dining table beside his and Jane's plate pleased John's eyes so much that his lips took up a crescent form. It was contrary to his expectation of finding George's plate on the floor.

The longer he looked at George's plate lying on the table adjacent to his, the wider became the smile on his face; it was a sign of his satisfaction with Jane, who looked at George not as a dog but a member of their family.

John's eyes were focused on the vegetable with tomato sauce and salmon and after few seconds, he uttered, "What a beautiful dish to look at." Jane turned her head with astonishment. The last two months, no matter what the dish was composed of, John's look at it triggered a nausea, causing him to refuse eating it. The sentence 'what a beautiful dish' sounded like music to her ears.

The real magic started when John grabbed a fork and a knife and began eating, off and on looking toward George, who was nibbling on his brat.

Jane wasn't in a hurry to forward the food into her stomach; her attention was focused on John. The small pieces he took, chewed and swallowed was a sight she was eager to see for the last two months, but it remained what it was, a wishful thinking. Now, her wish had materialized and she herself was the witness to the miracle.

The more she watched John, the more the preoccupation in her mind with the question: was that George who set in motion the event?

John finished his plate. With one hand, he was rubbing his stomach and the other ran through George's head, who had just cleaned out his plate.

He was so gratified with the food he had just consumed voluntarily after months of nausea that the smell of food prompted in him – that he couldn't change or stop the sentence which jumped out of his mouth – it was delicious. John's glance at George's plate brought back the exultation he felt when he realized George was being treated as a family member and not as a dog.

CHAPTER FIFTEEN

Meanwhile, Jane's desire to be without John or George's presence was growing, and after half an hour she gave in to it and announced that she felt tired and exhausted and wanted to go to bed to rest.

Once in the bedroom, she stretched herself in bed and turned off the bright light. Though mentally worn out, she couldn't escape thinking about George. She was aware of John's fondness for dogs, but that one day a dog will displace her in John's mind had never occurred to her.

The images of John being enthralled in George kept entering her mind and she asked herself: how can a dog have such magical power over a human? Or was she exaggerating the situation?

She pulled the blanket up to her chin and closed her eyes. Her attempt to fall asleep failed. No matter how the events of the day had drained her, the images of John holding George tightly, John running his fingers through his head while eating, John's eyes fixed at George for a long time, kept entering her mind.

Her attempt to block them by not focusing on the day's episode was unsuccessful. That is when the wave of fatigue took her to the ocean of sleep and by the time John arrived, she was drowned in it.

John glimpsed at her before lying in bed with his right arm wrapped around George. He could feel the energy entering his body through his arm. He was so relaxed with George at his side that he fell in the lap of slumber.

John opened his eyes. The brightness in the room heralded the beginning of a new day.

He extended his right arm immediately to the right to grab George. It touched the side few times and failed to discover George or any furry part. He turned his head; his eyes registered an empty side. He looked around; his eyes couldn't catch the sight of George anywhere, neither on the floor nor on Jane's bedside. He quickly jumped out of the bed to search for George. That is when a piece of paper attached to the nightstand with scotch tape attracted his attention. He ripped it off the nightstand so violently that the lamp on the stand started to shake.

He started reading, 'Hon, when I got up this morning you were in sound sleep, I thought you might crush him if you turn. I took him downstairs and he is resting on the couch. After so many troubled nights, seeing you sleeping soundly made an immense effect on me and the faint grin on your face suggested a pleasant dream, love you, Jane.'

The flight of stair leading to the first floor was made out of mahogany. John had to take few breaks while descending. The sweeping scent of mahogany in the air settled in his lungs. For a moment, he thought he was walking in the factory where the finely shaped balustrades for the railing were being manufactured, or was the scent coming from the narrow street flanked by mahogany trees and ending with the couch where George was resting?

He walked toward the couch. George's big eyes moved and were fixed at John's face.

He lifted him up into his chest. The warmth entering his body increased his vigorousness and vitality.

John felt the grumbling in his stomach, a sense which was evaporated from his memory, for he never paid attention to it, but this time his feeling was different. He petted George's head and uttered, "We are going to have a good breakfast."

In the kitchen, the bowl filled to the rim with cereal, banana, blueberries and milk looked so inviting, a spoonful found its way into John's mouth instead of George, the intended one, and pleased John's taste buds so much that he divided the bowl in two.

When they finished their breakfast, not a single flake of cereal could be found in George's bowl.

"I didn't know you were so fond of cereal." Though John missed the sound of woof in George, he could read the great satisfaction in his eyes.

He lifted George into his chest. The pleasant warmth which increased his vitality started creeping into John's body, which made John to lay his head on George's. A few minutes passed before George moved his head and glanced at John with the question in his eyes, "What is next?"

John looked at George for a second and said, "How about a walk?"

George had to struggle to separate himself from John and jumped on the table, directly looking at John's face as if saying, "No objection."

They walked jointly toward the entrance door.

John threw a look toward George and said, "I don't think you will need a leash."

John knew it was going to be cold when he opened the door. The winter was just a few weeks away. A cold wind blew in and reached his bone and made him to put his winter coat on top of his pullover and winter shirt. His glance at George must have convinced him that his fur was a good barrier of cold and they stepped out.

They passed by the ancient oak. Its size was still awesome, despite having lost almost all the leaves. It got out of his mind when they reached the crossing. There were just few cars passing, their low engine noise a testimonial to the posted twenty miles per hour speed limit.

Once the streets were void of cars, they got to the other side and continued walking along the side of the street.

After five minutes, they hit a narrow street and turned left. ¬Except for a passerby now and then, the street was deserted.

They were walking for almost five minutes when an elderly woman passed by, and her questioning eyes threw a look at George and John.

John guessed she must have been from the neighborhood and had not seen John or Jane walking with a dog.

Meanwhile, John turned left to walk toward the main parallel road. John's eyes screened the road; there were no souls or cars visible. The quiet and peacefulness of the street made John feel as if walking in a private garden with George. It had never crossed his mind that the mere presence of George was enough to take him to places he had never been before, like this garden full of flowers.

John was brought back to the street when his auditory system registered the woman, who was petting George and saying, "What a lovely dog. Dogs make a family complete. What is his name?"

"His name is George," John responded.

She must have known John's family, and that they didn't possess a dog until recently. George was indeed a member of the family, as revealed by Jane on his first day at home.

The concern which hit John's mind were people's eyes. They looked at him as a dog who had completed the family.

John's mind was preoccupied with someone whose arrival had an effect on his health, and he had felt the steady improvement of his condition since he lived with him.

Back at home, John's eyes screened the living room for a resting place for himself and George and, after a long search, decided that the couch was an ideal place. The large window, which offered the view of the ancient oak tree with its branches almost void of all its leaves as an indication of the coming winter, was across from it.

He took a seat on the couch and lifted George into his chest. The immediate enhancement of his vigorousness must have decreased his auditory sense, since it didn't record the clicking of the key in the entrance. It was the end of the school day and Jane was coming home.

When the door opened, he turned his head to the foyer and saw Jane.

The relatively loud voice, unusual for John, broke the silence in the living room. "Hi, Jane, how was school?"

"Not bad, but I am glad it is over and I can spend my time with you, that is why I didn't come through the garage," she stated.

She entered the living room. Before doing anything else, her eyes got fixed at John – lying on the couch and holding George in his chest – as if she was trying to decipher the secret of John's attachment to George. A few seconds passed. Her head moved toward John with a big smile; by all accounts, she wanted to please John, knowing the bond between him and George was strong, so she went ahead and asked, "When are we going for a walk with the dog?"

John didn't return her smile but got up and put George on

the floor and, with a voice full of ire and elements of correcting Jane's statement, said, "It is not a walk with the dog, it is a walk with George."

Jane stood there like somebody who was speechless, staring at John.

The word dog never appeared in her sentences whenever she was referring to George.

John opened his eyes to greet the new day. The bright sunshine had illuminated the entire room. Through the window, he saw the ancient oak tree. Its branches were not moving; the lack of even faint wind in the calm weather had a soothing effect on his mind. What was more soothing was the aroma of the air he was breathing in. He had noticed a perfume in the air since arrival of George. His look diverted to the bedside, where George was resting, his new place of resting, actually Jane's idea. His fell attracted his glance for a long time, as if he was looking at the site of the perfume production. The idea hit his mind to ask him if the aroma was coming from him, and the deeper he looked at George, the more intense and profound the aroma in the air became. At one point, the feeling of not being in the room but in a garden with a plethora of flower and bushes, their aroma penetrating the air, overcame him. He was asking himself if he was in the garden or was lost somewhere which exuded perfume.

For a while, he thought the aroma was a perception of his olfactory senses and not real, just an illusion, and George a puppy, a lovely one with two large dark eyes, and had nothing to do with the George of his medical school years. That is when the coin dropped, and he found out what he thought was the solution. Why not ask Jane? Her nose was certainly packed with olfactory nerve endings like anybody else, but her mind was not an easy prey for illusions of scent perception. Suddenly, Jane's statement of few weeks ago revived in his brain. He remembered the day communicating with Jane about thinking of quitting chemotherapy. That she believed some chemotherapy agents could alter the mind, which was not meant to discourage him. Jane's statement now had a different meaning to him and asking Jane if she perceived the aroma in the air started to worry him.

Better not ask her, lest she thinks his brain has gone awry, he thought.

It took him almost a minute to abandon the easy solution idea.

He took up George and walked slowly to the window. He felt again the warmth of George settling in his body. It wasn't like hugging an animal and feeling his warmth; the comforting effect was unknown to John.

The comfort, the return of his appetite, the enjoying of the food which he had lost: all were entangling his brain. He had lost his appetite for food, but he was enjoying his dishes again and all happened since George's arrival. It could also be a matter of coincidence, which happened after he had quit the treatment, he thought.

He walked toward the kitchen with George in his arms. Once in the kitchen, he put George on the counter. He was reflecting on what would be a good breakfast for George. His lips went up in a crescent form and he turned his head toward George. "Your fondness for cereal didn't escape my mind, but today I am preparing a different kind of breakfast for you."

He started slicing salami and turkey, alternating each with green vegetable on a white plate as if he was competing for an exam to become a chef.

George devoured the food. It looked like the presentation

had increased his appetite and hunger.

John turned to the bowl of cereal, raisin and fruits filled with milk. He was aware of George's fondness for cereal, but this bowl was destined to stop his hunger pangs, which recurred more often since George's arrival.

Meanwhile, the smell of coffee he had started to brew wafted in the air.

John threw a glance at George while the brown liquid was flowing into his stomach. In a matter of few minutes, the caffeine had perked him so up that the first thing to enter his mind was to go for a walk.

He looked at George and said, "I feel more power in my legs now, it is enticing me to go for a walk. Let's go."

The cold but crisp day enhanced his enthusiasm for the morning walk, but it didn't obscure his observation of George's behavior.

His decreased passion for a walk was obvious when a passerby petted his head and the satisfaction in his eyes which was always a source of pleasure for John was missing. George wasn't doing the walk to bring some excitement to John, he was following him as if he was trained in a dog school.

The walk intensified John's vigor and George was just following. John turned his eyes toward him like questioning his origin.

When they reached the front porch of John's house, he lifted him into his arms, ran his fingers into his head and said, "It doesn't look like you are having much fun today." He looked him straight into his eyes and asked – of course, without expecting an answer – "Where are you coming from?"

Back at home, John enhanced his tranquility by pushing Brahms piano concerto one into the CD player and, as soon as the sound started undulating in the air, he stretched himself on the couch. George's eyes were shut, his muzzle resting on his stretched forelegs. It looked he had fallen into the darkness of sleep, at the side of the couch. John assumed it was a good remedy for George, whose behavior today had similarities with a sick dog.

John's mind was entangled in thoughts trying to attribute his quick recovery to the arrival of George. On the other side, he was a doctor and the condition called spontaneous remission, the time when the patient is free of his or her infliction independent of type of treatment, was nothing new to him, but John was more inclined to ascribe it to the presence of George.

He took a deep breath and inhaled the heavenly scent of the air, for him a proof that the scent emanated from George.

John was exuberant about his new health and energy. John Zangonini, who had dedicated his life to his work, was being reborn. He had mounted a rocky hill and now was entering a garden with tall trees, green bushes and flowers with different color. The wasteland of cancer was conquered. He wasn't dreaming, these were actual facts, he thought. He looked to the side where George was resting, and his face glittered with gratitude.

John's head was resting on the palms of his hands. He had shut his eyes and was absorbing the Brahms tune in the air. The peaceful ambiance was shattered by the pounding of high heels on the wooden floor of foyer, followed by Jane's voice. "Hon, my school is over."

She tucked the chair across from the couch, perched her behind on it and looked at John. Her school day must have been very stressful, since the first sentence coming out of her mouth was, "I am glad the school is over. I couldn't have tolerated it one more hour," and continued with the same voice, "How was your day?"

"The walk with George was refreshing as usual," he responded but his eyes appeared questioning – *is that your real question?*

He stared at her, the expression on his face read *just fire away what is in your mind, I am open to everything.*

Jane's eyes were fixed at him, as if his response or whatever was in his mind wasn't important to her. She was searching for words to formulate her statement, which seemed significant to her. Eventually, she overcame her hesitation and gave up on finding out John's reaction to her announcement.

"I have a plan for this evening," came right out of her mouth with a firm voice. "After we have finished our routines, we go out for dinner with George." She kept staring at John before continuing with the same firm voice, "I have made a reservation at Colbeh restaurant."

"Fantastic," came out of John's mouth like a shot. John continued. He sounded enthusiastic. "To hear the name Colbeh added fire to my desire to sit with you and George and have dinner there."

John looked straight in her eyes and continued, "As a matter of fact, I called the restaurant to make a reservation, only to find that the next available table was in six weeks, which deterred me so much that I gave up. I am flabbergasted that you got a table on such short notice."

Jane responded right away, "It was a cancellation which made it possible."

John chuckled and said, "Let's cross the tiled way to the restaurant together this evening."

Jane missed the many people in a restaurant. To be among

them again was one of her longings she thought will never come true. John's condition had improved so much that the obstacles John used as an excuse for not going for dinner didn't exist anymore and she was emboldened to call the restaurant.

CHAPTER SIXTEEN

She was on her way to cafeteria to join her colleagues for lunch. John had not talked to her about his infliction with cancer yet.

A chair was kept empty for her as usual. She perched on the chair.

She couldn't participate in the conversation; they were talking about Colbeh restaurant. Shirly, one of her colleagues, couldn't put a clamp on her enthusiasm about her entrée in the restaurant. "The grilled salmon was placed on spinach which was treated with white wine and encircled with colorful vegetables. It looked like a piece of art. When it touched my palate, I had to ask myself: what were the spices making it so delicious?"

She was raving about the food when Jane looked at her with a faint enthusiasm on her face and said, "I have to try it," hoping she will end her ravings about the food at Colbeh. A fleeting glance of Shirly at her was all it brought about, and she continued, "And the dessert, the chocolate brownie, is something to die for. Don't forget to order it right with your entrée, otherwise you have to wait for it thirty minutes, since they make it from scratch. But it will please your palate so much, it is worth the wait." Her admiration for Colbeh went on, as if she wanted to brag that she could afford to spend an evening there.

A forced grin appeared on Jane's face and she apologized for leaving early to complete her unfinished work. She elevated her butt from the chair and said, "I have to try it," and left.

John's recovery had sped up since George's arrival. Every morning when she woke up and looked at John, he was soundly asleep, something she had missed for a couple of months. When returning from school, John's actions reminded her of the time he was cancer-free. It looked he had finally conquered the demon who was out to destroy him; he even talked to her few days earlier about thinking to go back to work.

That is when the images of her colleagues in the busy cafeteria reappeared in her mind. Shirly was raving about the secrets of the grilled salmon and its pleasing effects on her palate. It was a joy watching John chew on some salmon; the way his eyes were glittering was a revelation of pleasure. To watch him chew the delicious Colbeh salmon must be like a new experience, she thought. Besides, she will have the opportunity to intermingle with a lot of people. John's recovery gave her the entitlement to call Colbeh. For a while, she had second thoughts. She knew through John of patients with cancer who experienced a spontaneous remission and relapsed after few months, or was John's recovery really related to George's arrival? She let her belief in coincidence to take over and extended her arm to the phone receiver and dialed Colbeh for a reservation.

Colbeh had conquered the town in a short time and became its most famous, but also most expensive restaurant.

Guests sang praises of its entrées and desserts. Special occasions like birthdays or anniversaries were reasons most people turned a blind eye on the financial burden it placed on their budget.

The obligatory wait of at least a month didn't have any deterring effect on her; it actually worked as an additional attraction. Her excitement was almost overwhelming when she heard a table was available for the same day due to cancellation, which she perceived as if music from paradise was sounding in her ears.

CHAPTER SEVENTEEN

The chef of Colbeh was introduced to subtleties of cooking under a three stars chef. Meticulous attention and hard work helped him to master the skills. The concept of being a master chef in his own restaurant was a constant occupier of his mind since.

One day while driving home, he came across an empty building with adjacent parking lot with a for sale sign.

He got out of his car and walked around the building, peeked into the windows and found it would work for his new venture, according to his imagination. A month later, he was renovating and furnishing it.

Large windows in the dining hall allowed for sweeping views of surrounding houses with their gabled roofs and the greeneries around the few small hills. The antique tables and chairs blended well with the paintings and art objects decorating the walls and were often a good distraction for guests who might have been vexed due to delays with their food.

He bought a massive oak door with leaded glass for the entrance, which enhanced in some guests the expectation of a fine dining experience.

John drove the car toward Colbeh restaurant. Jane was sitting on the shotgun seat with George on her lap. John's right hand frequently ran through George's head and neck. They approached the parking lot. He left the car on the side of the lot, took George into his chest and hugged him tightly, and they walked toward the entrance of the restaurant.

A tall man in a black suit, whose tight sitting white shirt outlined his beefy pectoralis, welcomed them at the entrance. "HI, you have a reservation?" he asked.

"A table for Zangonini," John responded.

After a quick look in the reservation book, the tall man beckoned them toward the dining hall. While walking them to the hall, all of a sudden, his glance took notice of George, who was walking beside John.

"Sorry you can't take the dog with you," he said very politely and continued, "but we have a special room for pets and—"

He couldn't finish his sentence, since John interrupted him abruptly. "He is not a dog," he uttered, obviously spontaneous and without any reflection.

…he couldn't finish his sentence, since John interrupted him abruptly. "He is not a dog," he uttered, obviously spontaneous and without any reflection.

The tall receptionist had a hard time to suppress the smirk on his face and insisted on his words, "Sorry, no dogs are allowed in the dining hall."

It was apparent that it was difficult for the tall man to express himself calmly. John was ruffled up and came a step closer to the tall man and said in a raised voice, "I told you, George is not a…"

John had to stop and turn his head toward Jane, whose left hand was squeezing John's right arm so forcefully that the only way to release himself from the squeeze was to turn around and remove Jane's hand.

His questioning eyes were asking, "Jane, why are you hurting me?"

When his glance hit Jane's face, he stopped immediately addressing the tall man. Her eyes and her face were pointing toward the exit.

The threesome walked out quietly; to announce anything seemed to be superfluous. John was silent but a turmoil was raging in his mind. It centered around the tall man. Without Jane's squeeze, it would have been easy to bring down the receptionist to his knees, he was thinking, and it wasn't easy for John to disentangle his brain from the idea.

He tossed a glance at Jane, who had to stop him by using force. The thought of being so stupid to ruin a promising evening engulfed his brain but he remained silent.

George was walking beside him like a faithful companion and not like a fair-weather friend. There was no escape not looking at him and enjoying its calming effect.

It was an empty bench on the restaurant lot which was the trigger for John's lips to move. "Let's have a seat," he said.

Their behinds felt the cold and hard surface of the bench, but their thick winter coat kept them comfortable. John threw a glance at George's fell and thought it was a good protector against the cold.

The blue sky was stained in some areas by moving small clouds which couldn't compete with the countless sparkling stars and the full moon bragged with its beauty whenever it was uncovered by the moving clouds. Through the gabled roofs, the moonshine penetrated to make the shadows of tall trees visible. The hilly park-like location of the restaurant made their eyes fixed at the infrequent passing of the cars in the narrow streets of the neighborhood.

After a while, John's eyes diverted to Jane and tossed a look at her. He said, after a second, how sorry he was to have ruined the nice evening in the famous restaurant and said, "For sure, we can enjoy Colbeh another time." He went on, "The receptionist was insisting that George was a..."

He couldn't finish his sentence and paused while his eyes moved toward George. His look at George was bursting with love and lingered for half a minute before he diverted them toward Jane.

One way for John to figure out Jane's reaction to his statement to the receptionist that George wasn't a dog was to study her eyes and her face. Jane's eyes were staring into space as if searching for something lost and her face didn't describe anything: this was his interpretation.

It didn't help John, who was struggling with the idea to spill the reasons of his mind why George wasn't a dog. He kept screening her eyes but with more deliberation. At the end, his courage caught up with him and his mouth moved while his eyes were straightly looking into hers "Do you believe in guardian angels?"

The question shattered Jane in a way that an explosion of a bomb in front of a person will do. It destroyed John's images residing in her mind.

John the agnostic, the naturalist, to whom the universe was nature and not a creation as presented by the holy book.

His answer to explain that the universe was the result of a primordial explosion which was still unfolding was that it was something not explainable by ratio.

The explanation of the creation as presented by the holy book came from kingdom of God. Then the kingdoms were governing the world. He had tried many times to make clear that the heavenly kingdom was the creation of man; since the world was dominated by kingdoms, it was easy to create a heavenly kingdom, which is understood by people. Now the same John who made fun of being rewarded or punished in the afterlife is referring to God's angels and apparently considers George coming from there.

It looked that the veil in front of her eyes was all of a sudden torn and she could view the true John.

John's recovery started with the arrival of George. What about the spontaneous remission she had heard John talking about her patients?

Is that just a matter of coincidence?

It was actually George who took off the veil from her eyes and unveiled to her the true John, and the whole thing took just a few seconds to play in her mind.

The idea that George was an angel was so solidly anchored in John's mind and wasn't just a phantasy of him. She thought that she didn't want to uproot it, though she was aware of the fact that any of her attempts would be futile. She pursed her lips and put them on John's cheek, who was running his fingers in George's head. John felt the warmth of her breath which penetrated his body. It didn't affirm his thought, but soothed his entire frame. A calmed-down John watching the infrequent traffic on the streets below vouched for it.

After few minutes, John broke the silence. "It is getting dark, let's get something to eat," was his utterance.

The walk down the hill was quiet but refreshing. After ten minutes, they came across an eatery which looked more like a fast-food joint to them.

John threw a look through the window at the counter-top where the food was displayed. His view lingered on the containers filled with fresh vegetables. The fish and slices of turkey were arranged on a flat tray with a freshly grilled chicken lying beside them, but to John, the French baguettes which looked newly fetched out of the oven looked irresistible. John didn't continue to explore the food. He turned his head toward Jane and said, "I don't think George demurs turkey meat."

They entered the restaurant. Out of twenty vinyl-topped round tables, half were unoccupied. They chose one by the window. The turkey sandwiches layered with a lot of vegetables tasted delicious.

When they were done, John took a sip of his lime flavored mineral water, dabbed his stomach with a content face and said "I don't think at Colbeh I would have been more satisfied," which was contrary to Jane's facial expression of lamenting a destroyed evening in a famous restaurant.

Back at home, the three of them were relaxing in the living room on the couch. George was perching beside John.

It was the air John was inhaling which elevated his spirit and zest for life, he was convinced of it.

He turned his head toward Jane and almost asked her if she felt the same, but his intuition of her mourning the lost evening made him abandon the idea quickly.

He lifted George into his arms, set him on his lap and started petting him.

Jane threw a glance toward John and, while yawning, said, "I am tired and I am going to bed."

"A good idea," was John's response. "I will join you later."

When he entered the bedroom a little later, Jane was standing on the bedside. Her blouse laid on the bed, her bra still on. Her hair covered almost the entire nape of her neck, as if trying to compete with the smooth skin of her back.

John approached her quietly and wrapped his arms around her neck. His hands grabbed her breasts gently and he whispered into her ears, "I love you."

She responded with a voice on the lower side, "I have loved you since our first encounter."

His lips started their slow journey on her body, kissing her ears, lips, breasts, until they reached her legs. The warmth of her skin was piercing into his body deeply and made him feel weightless and floating.

John lifted her into the bed. Both undressed completely and kissed so passionately, like two lovers who had not seen each other for a long time, and when they became one and entered the seventh heaven, the events of the past evening evaporated.

The bright sunshine made the warm bedroom so sunny, betraying the cold weather outside. Occasionally, a walker appeared on the street and was wrapped up well in winter coat, and some had to carry a hat, too.

John's eyes were focused on the ancient oak tree outside. He moved his right hand toward the right side of the bed where George had found his resting place for the night, and started petting his head and, after few moments, turned his head toward him and uttered in a low voice, "Today we are going to jog after breakfast."

Their stomachs filled with milk, cereal and fruits, and a heavy winter coat making John appear wider, they headed to the street.

The cold weather triggered a faster jogging in John, and it was hard for George to keep pace with him. For John, George was in very good shape. He took the vapor flowing out of George's mouth as a sign of his enjoyment.

Back home, though he wanted to surprise Jane with dinner, he still missed the sound of music for unwinding. He was very pleased once the CD he had pushed into the player started emitting the sound of Beethoven's emperor sonata.

He expected Jane in few hours, but preparing dinner for three had made his mind preoccupied with cooking. He put the recipe and chose all the ingredients and placed them on the countertop. In the kitchen, the emperor sonata caressed his auditory nerves. The ingredients and recipe already on the counter-top, his mind was getting ready to perform an easy job.

John Zangonini started like an experienced chef. He added a cup of rice to two cups of water and half a teaspoon of salt, let it boil without ever looking at it again. Meanwhile, sliced mushrooms and shallots were sizzling in the frying pan, and he added pieces of chicken breast at his discretion, along with herbs he had already measured before.

He tossed a glance at George and stated, "It looks that we are going to have a fine dinner."

CHAPTER EIGHTEEN

For Jane, the arrival of George was a burden which would weigh in on her, who had already reached the breaking point.

After the stresses of the school, her arrival at home was marked by a husband who had returned from chemo or radiation lying on the couch while classical music echoed in the air. The added trouble of a dog made her to get closer to the breaking point. She deliberately missed cafeteria to avoid her colleagues, though the sandwiches she brought to consume for lunch pleased her palate more than cafeteria food.

Her steps took additional speed whenever passing by colleagues to eschew their puzzled faces. Sometimes the feeling of a nightmare will overcome her, but the realization of reality was just a matter of few seconds.

Nonetheless, after few days of George's arrival, she was flabbergasted by John's health changing rapidly for the better. His enjoyment of life was obvious, and she had to give up urging him to take something into his stomach. Not only had his appetite returned, he was eating his breakfast, lunch and dinner like a hungry person.

It was a welcome change for Jane, who attributed it to a spontaneous remission, a condition in which the symptoms of a disease disappear independent of treatment, and she got familiar with it when, in the past, John talked about his cancer patients.

The change was very welcome to her and to attribute it to George's arrival would be eerie, she thought. The word *coincidence* had not disappeared from her vocabulary.

Though she was inclined to attribute John's improvement to a spontaneous remission, all the same, George had occupied a special place in her heart. It could be that she never kicked away the notion, and the association of George with John's improvement still lingered in her mind.

The image of John holding George tightly or sitting beside him, caressing his head, had become a familial factor for her whenever returning home after a taxing day at the school. Jane's behavior at the school had already started to change; she had started her lunch breaks at the cafeteria and trying to avoid her colleagues whenever passing them never occurred again. The whispering among her colleagues continued that whoever she was consulting was solving her marital problems.

December arrived with a very cold day. The sun had disappeared behind the stagnant clouds, the sky had dropped and the way people were clothed was testimony to the freezing weather. The dreary weather had no impact on John's mind, which was intertwisted with images of himself wearing a white gown examining a patient, or in a meeting with some colleagues or even he was in a gathering with Martin again. Those days of chemo and radiation nausea and dry mouth were buried by George. John was sure George had destroyed the daemon who had ravaged his body and given him his physical condition back.

He looked at the calendar; it was Wednesday, a perfect day to restart his lunch meetings with Martin and let him to be the first who listens to the announcement of him intending to open his office again.

It took only few seconds to overcome the initial hesitation and he grabbed the phone and dialed Martin's number.

He was certain Martin would recognize his voice; nevertheless, he announced, "HI, here is John."

Martin did recognize it, though the puzzle in his voice gave away the unexpected surprise of him. "I am glad you are back to normal. But I never thought your recovery would be so fast."

His loud laugh following the statement manifested his genuine joy about the news.

John, unable to suppress his chuckle, responded, "We will have a lot to talk about. I can't hardly wait until noon arrives and we meet again in our restaurant."

Martin detached his butt from the surface of his chair as soon as his eyes located John. John walked with accelerated pace toward him and the two hugged tightly, like two friends meeting after a long sabbatical. When they unhugged and perched on their chairs, Martin's eyes screened John from top to bottom, again and again, as if he was evaluating a rare object.

His glance was still lingering on John when he broke the silence. "To be honest, I never expected to see you in such a good shape in such a short time."

John's lips assumed the shape of early moon, then moved to express his feelings. "I feel very well; actually, I feel cured and intend to resume my practice again very soon." He went on after a brief pause, "I am looking forward to our Wednesday lunch meeting."

Martin poured the Malbec, their favorite wine, into their glasses. They raised them and simultaneously said, "To our continuous friendship," and Martin added, just before drinking, "And to your new start"

CHAPTER NINETEEN

The department of obstetrics and gynecology of the hospital comprised twenty attendings who met regularly the last Friday of each month to discuss the old and new business of the department and set new policies in effect, if needed. John was absent from the meetings and the hospital for three months. Any attending who was absent for over three months – except for vacation – had to formally apply for renewal of her or his privileges at the department, according to the policies of the department.

John had the chairman already know of his intention to restart his practice. At the end of the meeting and after the old and new business of the department were discussed, the chairman announced that John was disease-free and would be resuming his duties. A round of applause followed the announcement and made a feeling of embarrassment creep into John. He always was discomforted when the applause was for him; nevertheless, he stood up to show his appreciation. The meeting adjourned and John walked with slow steps toward the parking lot.

It was a gloomy day. It looked like the sun had lost its intention to reappear from its resting place behind the dark clouds and infuse some comfort into the cold air. Though the announcement of his return had warmed him up, nevertheless he had to accelerate his steps.

In the car, the thought of George running toward him, wagging his tail gave him more energy. It had engrossed him so much that he pressed the gas pedal immediately and directed the car toward home.

He entered the living room. George was lying on the couch. He didn't run toward him. His body was stretched on the couch and his head was resting on his forelegs. His eyes started opening very slowly as John approached him and started to pet him.

When he tossed a tired look at John, the idea that something might not be in order with him slowly started creeping into his mind, but he quickly wiped it out, ran his fingers through his head and said, "You would be nimble again as soon as your throat comes in touch with your favorite food," and headed toward the kitchen. The scent of the cut salmon reached the air in the living room, but George's head was resting motionless on his forelegs.

The sliced salmon on a white plate in one hand and a porcelain bowl filled with water in the other hand, he approached George. The placement of the plates in front of him didn't move his head, instead his eye lids went up very slowly but went down again as if conveying to John the message, "Don't make me chew and swallow those red sausages."

John recalled George had difficulty to slide down his chew recently. After the flagrance of salmon in the air revealed no effect on him and he was indirectly refusing to eat, the concept of taking him to a vet entered his mind.

John wrapped his arms around George, lifted him up, his eyes overflowing with love. He moved toward the large window of the living room. The ancient oak tree, with branches void of any leaves, was looking at him like an old friend.

Though the view of his oak tree had attracted his attention, his thoughts were entangled with George's reluctance to touch his food. His eyes fixed at the branches of the oak tree brought back to him the experience he had with viruses. Often the first symptom it produced was loss of appetite; though it evolved his patients who were affected with a virus, nevertheless he thought it could do the same in a dog.

He pressed his cheek against George's head and told him, "Don't worry, it will be over in a few days."

The few days passed. Even though John succeeded to get some turkey meat down his throat with a lot of water to accompany it, George's condition didn't improve. That is when Ed entered his mind.

CHAPTER TWENTY

Ed was one of his classmates in high school, a smart guy, reserved and self-absorbed. During lunch break, he often wasn't present in the cafeteria but in the library, lost in books dealing with animals, apparently more important to him than socializing in cafeteria. John's friendship with Ed was firmly established since he discussed with him the subject of animal cruelty.

On the sunny and warm day in May, he was on his way home and was admiring the blue sky, totally free of even specks of white, when suddenly a white spot in the sky attracted his attention. It was a pigeon busy tumbling, as if the sun and the blue sky encouraged the summersaulting, or was the pigeon just displaying its zest for life?

It fascinated John so much that he didn't notice the falcon, who was approaching the pigeon with lightning speed without flapping its wings.

The bird of prey was flying back with the pigeon firmly held in its paws, white feathers flying around in its wake. That shocked John beyond perception. He was simply overwhelmed. The image of a pigeon falling prey to a falcon was so powerful, it pushed aside all other thoughts in his mind.

In the darkness of the night, the image of a blue sky with a pigeon, drunken with life, grabbed by a falcon, white feathers flying around in its wake, appeared again and again in his dreams.

The next day, John stumbled upon Ed in the locker room.

His knowledge of animals, the time he spent to study their behavior was an open secret to him. He turned to him right away.

"HI, Ed, it might surprise you, but your inclination to animals and your readings about their behavior makes me think you are the one on the ball for my question."

Ed glimpsed at him with a puzzled face without mentioning a word and John went on to describe the falcon attack of the pigeon.

He added, "The brutality of the attack was so vivid that I can't take it off my mind. I have tried not to think about it, but the picture keeps returning to my mind."

Ed was doing his best to conceal his contempt for someone who considered the bird of prey's way of life a brutality. He responded with a smile on his face, "I wouldn't call it a brutality but a necessity." He went on, "the birds of prey feed on other birds because they provide the food for them and their babies."

His face and his eyes exhibited signs of patronizing; his eyes, especially, were glittering with wisdom when his mouth continued carrying the talk, "We kill other animals for eating, God didn't place us on earth as vegetarians."

John had come across Ed in cafeteria quite often, but the sight of him being involved in a lively discussion with Ed was not just rare but unique.

John thanked Ed for the information. Ed's love for animals had downed him a place in the vet school. He announced his acceptance in the veterinary school to be the happiest day in his life. He didn't mention the countless hours he had spent in the library studying animal life.

Ed's busy veterinary clinic was a fifteen-minute drive from John's residence. A surprised but pleasant voice welcomed him when his call was connected to his office. Ed had recognized John's voice right away.

"Hi, John, how are you? I haven't talked to you for a long time."

John responded, "Hi…" and few moments of silence passed before he continued, "There have been some changes in my life which I would like to talk about later. The reason I am calling you now is George." The ensuing silence made Ed guess John was reflecting on his next sentence as how to present George. John broke his silence by quickly declaring that George was his dog.

Ed noticed his reluctance to talk about his dog, so he tried to give him more time. "I didn't know you had a dog," he responded.

He had hardly finished his sentence when John jumped in. "Well, I don't consider George my dog, but my friend." Then, he continued with a calm voice, "George has lost his appetite and has become lethargic. He spewed out his last bite and—"

"I would see him today, if you had a chance to bring him in," Ed interrupted John before he was able to finish.

The interruption was considered by John as a proof of having made the right decision.

Approximately one hour later, one of the seats in Ed's waiting room was occupied by John, with George resting in his lap. Next to him, the seat was taken by a cage accommodating a blue parrot, obviously belonging to the middle-aged woman sitting next to it. Her big smile greeted John when he was about to occupy his seat.

The seat across from John was accommodated by a man who was concealed behind a magazine and was so absorbed in it that he didn't notice John's arrival. His big white Labrador looked tired and exhausted. The eyes of the dog were right away fixed at George and after a short while, he got up and slowly moved toward George and, when he approached him, started sniffling at George. He was testing his readiness to engage in a play.

George's upper lids moved slowly upwards. His attempt to open them was completely unsuccessful and they fell down again, oblivious to the sniffling of the Labrador. His owner put his magazine away. His puffed-up face tossed an indifferent glance at John and took his dog back to its place.

While John was looking at the Labrador, the door of the examining room flung open. An average size man with thick framed black glasses was glimpsed at the waiting area. The moment his eyes hit John, he approached him.

"You haven't changed since I saw you last time," he stated while shaking John's hands.

"Neither have you, nice to see you again," was John's response.

John wanted to get to the heart of the matter right away.

"Well, I talked to you about George's condition over the phone," he uttered.

"Yes" answered Ed, his right hand on John's right shoulder. He continued, "Come into the examining room and we will talk about George".

Inside Ed's exam room, he perched on the chair across from him with George on his lap and Ed's desk between them. After a glimpse at Ed, he uttered, "George has become lethargic lately and he threw up his bite last time."

"Let me examine him," Ed responded.

John got up while lifting George into his chest. He pressed him tightly against his sternum and felt the warmth and energy raising in his body again. He pursed his lips and pressed them against his head.

A silent John watched Ed's stethoscope move over George's chest. Ed asked John to keep George's mouth open and had a look inside with his head mirror projecting light inside George's throat.

A layer of concern which didn't escape John's eyes covered his face. Looking into the mouth and throat of George from different angles added to the ominous lines on his face. After a moment, Ed petted George and, with love-filled eyes, looked straight into his eyes. It didn't, however, decrease the sense of premonition in John that Ed had come across something significant.

John was about to leave his seat and approach Ed and ask him if he had found something serious. Ed's face had become so grave, with his eyes fixed at George with concern, that John gave up, and rather waited to learn from Ed what he had found out.

Ed moved toward John with a face full of concern. His voice was calm but determined, something easy for John to discern. "John, it looks that your friend George has a tumor in his upper throat." He stared at John and continued, "It must be growing fast; I can look at it through his mouth and I might be able to grab it with a biopsy forceps and take a sample, if you consent to it. John was silent when he nodded his approval.

"I think local anesthesia will suffice, but if the need arises, he will be put under," he said.

John's glance at Ed was reminiscent of a man who was absent-minded. A few seconds of silence passed before he could utter under his breath, "Go ahead with local."

Ed lifted George into his chest and proceeded toward the operating room.

Half an hour later, he came back carrying George in his arms. ED's face was brimming with satisfaction. "The planned procedure ended up well," he announced to John. The biopsy turned out to be easy to perform and the bleeding could be controlled with coagulating gel.

He placed George on the examining table and said, "You can take him home whenever you are ready. I should have the biopsy result in about two to three days."

He approached John and gave him a light hug and stated, "When we meet again, we will have plenty of time to recount to each other the stories of our lives of the past couple of years."

Back home, he put George on the couch and uttered, "Rest will alleviate all the stress you went through today," and knelt next to the couch, starting to caress him on his back. George's eyes opened and he stared at John. If he could open his mouth, he would have reported that his journey to this world is nearing its end.

John's eyes were fixed at him. He felt the warmth inside his body without even touching him when he got on his feet again.

CHAPTER TWENTY-ONE

John was thinking to regain his privileges at the hospital. The rule of the department asked any attending who was away for more than three months to reapply for his reappointment, unless he or she was away for vacation. The chairman had to be notified before the meeting and the request would be part of new business of the department, and John was familiar with the rule.

The staff was discussing John's request for reappointment when the phone rang. The secretary who also recorded the minutes of the meeting picked it up. After a few seconds of listening, she handed it over to John. "It is your wife," she said.

John's heart dropped when he heard his wife was calling. Except for a very serious matter, Jane never called during his meeting hour. *Something is wrong with George* was the first thought hitting his mind, and a quick succession of horrible conditions George might be experiencing entangled his head.

"Hi, Jane, is George OK?" his trembling voice asked.

On the other side of the line, a voice which was trying hard to sound calm answered, "John, how are you?" And without waiting for a response, it continued, "I checked on George before leaving to see if I should prepare breakfast for him. He was extremely lethargic and wasn't capable of raising his eyelid, even though he was putting a lot of effort in it. I lifted his muzzle to check his eyelids and noticed specks of blood around his mouth. I am aware he underwent a biopsy in his mouth yesterday, which would explain the appearance of blood stains." A moment of silence broke her conversing and John thought she was trying to prevent her imminent crying. Once in control again, she continued with a higher voice, apparently to keep the quivering in her voice out, "I am calling you because I didn't know what to do".

Silence overcame John. He was holding the receiver with his left hand and his left biceps started twitching.

After a few seconds, a trembling voice aired through the line. "Just stay there, I will be home in ten minutes."

He returned the receiver to the secretary. His eyes gave him a blurred view of the chairman who was surveying him. The room was quiet and all eyes were riveted at him when he announced with calm voice that he had to leave because of an emergency. He scheduled his request for the next meeting and headed for the parking lot.

The wind lingered and had gained on strength. It was cold and it pierced through the clothing. John thought of an ice cube which was touching his bone. The faint sunshine trying to break through the cloud didn't distract the focus of John's attention. His mind was deeply engaged about George's bleeding source. Ed's mentioning of how easy it was to control the bleeding by a coagulating gel repeated itself again and again in his head. He was making the tumor on its own right the origin of the bleeding. The fast growth of the tumor can cause ulceration, or it can grow into the neighboring vessels and make him bleed. His heart started pounding when the thought entered his mind that he might bleed to death. His steps got faster and he got into his car. The head wind had almost disappeared, and after a while he felt his nostrils were transmitting a warm air to his lungs. What he didn't realize was that the heating was running full speed and he was speeding. The outline of his house loomed.

He entered the house. The scent of rose petals with their evaporating dews, the perfume emanating from George since his arrival, had evaporated. His memory of a heavenly warmth exuding from George's body to him whenever he held him awakened. Will he experience it again when he holds him in his arms?

His call for George reverberated in the air. There was no response; Jane, who saw John's approaching car through the window, had left as soon as the car came into her sight. She had never been tardy.

He approached the couch where George was lying. Through the large window, the ancient oak tree was showing off its leafless branches. A faint wind rustled through them and scattered some of the dried-up leaves on the ground.

His glance of the center of the couch kept him frozen. George was lying there, motionless. John had to give up his lingering look of his chest after a while. There was no detectable sign of any movement. George's eyes were completely shut.

John's premonition had become a reality. His assumption that the perfume in the air was coming from George was correct, he thought. And now the disappearance of the fragrance was the indication of his departure from the earth.

John's eyes were riveted at George's motionless body.

It took few moments for John to overcome his hesitance and touch George. It was cold. He lifted his limp head. He was crashed after his ear on George's chest didn't determine a beating heart, as the faint hope in his mind had pointed to.

A feeling of cold overwhelmed him. He felt wretched. George had departed from this world and will be, from now on, just a memory.

John's eyes were fixed at George's motionless body. He was

like a lost person in a room in which he was robbed of his life companion. Without George, his life had become an empty place. It was the ringing of the phone which reminded him that he wasn't completely left alone.

He turned his head toward the receiver and grabbed it.

"Can I talk to Dr. Zangonini?" Ed's voice sounded like Ed's voice on the receiver end.

"Hi, Ed, how are you doing?"

"Very well," he responded and went on, "I am calling regarding George's biopsy result." At this point, Ed paused, as if his break will reduce the effects of his bad news. After a short while, he continued, "I am sorry, John, to be the messenger of this depressing news; your friend George has squamous cell cancer in his upper throat."

John was silently looking into the receiver, his mind entangled in eerie thoughts. A few seconds of silence passed before John could respond. A mournful voice sounded in the phone, "I don't know how to thank you for all you have done for me. Right now I have to leave because of an emergency. I will talk to you soon regarding George," and hung up without waiting for an answer.

The questions creeping into John's mind were so eerie and unsettling that John pulled a chair to sit down. Squamous carcinoma of the upper throat is what he was inflicted with. The same cancer is reappearing in George and killing him, while he got steady improvement of his. Did he come to absorb John's ailment into his body? All the boost in energy and warmth he felt whenever holding him were to pull his cancer into his body? He sat on the chair for a long time and couldn't disentangle his thoughts. Minutes passed before he found the composure to get up and approach George. He lifted the lifeless body. While holding him tightly in his chest, he put his head over George's and stood there motionless for minutes.

He moved toward the couch and put George on it and set his behind on the couch adjacent to George. The events of last three months were ravaging his mind. He got sick and underwent chemotherapy and radiation and quit, just at the time of George's arrival. All the energy and warmth entering his body whenever he hugged him were explainable with— His line of thought was leading him to where miracles originate and he wasn't prepared to accept it. He turned his head, with eyes soaked in love, toward George. The idea had taken root in John's mind long before George's death. He was a big fantast, but the fantasy with George was so crazy that he tried very hard to eliminate it from his mind and he wasn't successful. His eyes gazed at George for a while; the thought of a cold place covered with earth where George will be resting was replacing his fantasy.

His struggle to find a resting place for George proved to be a tough one. Yellow pages were first to come to his mind. However, the idea faded quickly. Relying on an address book for a funeral place was like playing Russian roulette. What he needed was a recommendation based on a personal experience with a funeral home, where he can ask for the cold place for his beloved George. It was clear to him that the conception that George had absorbed his cancer so he walks as a person free of the sickness was insane, a fairy tale story. Human beings' flight of fantasies can go to the extreme and become delusional, he was aware of it. The idea, no matter how insane, had a firm place in his mind. His look moved toward George, whom he considered his savior. George must have a suitable resting place; the least he could do was to base the place on a recommendation. He had him in his sight while he was searching in the deep crevices of his brain for somebody who can recommend a funeral place. It turned out to be as difficult as looking for the holy grail. Suddenly his eyes twinkled. Talk to Sarah, she will have the recommendation.

CHAPTER TWENTY-TWO

Sarah was sixty years old when the angel of death picked up her husband, uprooted her life and put her at risk of getting axed.

Even two months thereafter, returning home from her work was like feeling the silence and calm of a cemetery, which worsened her depression.

Swallowing pills gave her some sleep, but the mug of strong black coffee in the morning didn't alleviate her fatigue and weariness.

Her manager, who had appreciated her devotion to her job and her contribution to the company in writing just few months prior to the untimely departure of her husband, had called her to his office.

"Sarah, I totally understand your big loss, but my job requires to direct my coworkers to focus on their routine. I plead with you to pay more attention to your duties and not to force me to look for a replacement," was his statement. She had promised her best, but, in actuality, nothing in her depressed condition pointed to that direction.

She came across his neighbor, Alena, the next day, who asked her if she knew anybody who could take her cat, because she was being transferred to Sydney and couldn't take her with.

"I am being transferred to Australia and want the best for my cat," she mentioned.

Sarah had been many times at Alena's, and had ran his fingers through her head and back while admiring her with the words, "What a lovely cat." Sarah knew somebody. She adopted the cat, Peace.

Caring for Peace didn't bring new routines to her life, it became her new life. Her depression gradually subsided and her reliance on sleeping pills decreased, as if, with Peace, life had returned to her.

Sarah used to visit John for her annual exam but more frequently she sat in the waiting room for her female problems. John recalled her cat because on the examining table she often digressed from her actual problems and talked about Peace. John had become accustomed to it. As a matter of fact, her digressions had made John very familiar with Peace, without having asked a single question about the cat.

Once, she didn't appear for her appointment without having cancelled it. A few days later, she called John and apologized for missing her appointment.

She had assured herself a place in John's mind as a diligent and dutiful person and not to show for an appointment indicated something serious. That is why his question about the reason for not showing at her scheduled appointment.

It was obvious that she was trying forcefully to avoid the trembling in her voice when she stated, "I had to go to the pet cemetery."

"A pet cemetery?" a puzzled voice responded from the other side of the line.

"I had to bury my cat, Peace. I woke up in the morning and found the lifeless body of Peace on the carpet where she was resting.

"What did you do with her?" John asked.

"At least I found a good resting place for her close to my house," was her response.

John couldn't have found a better recommendation. John scoured all the crevices in his brain for Sarah's residence and at the end of the day, didn't find a clue. But he knew Sarah's residence was close to his office, actually so close she always walked to perch in John's waiting room. Checking with the yellow pages for a close to his office pet cemetery revealed the pet cemetery which was close to his office. The cemetery was advertised to be a quiet place, and Sarah's words supported it. At last, a shining spot in the darkness of his tragedy. He turned his head, and after the look at the lifeless body of George reminded him of his desolate situation, he grabbed the phone and dialed the funeral home's number.

A friendly voice responded, "Funeral services for pets, how can I help you?"

"I would like to bury my pet today, and I know it is a short notice, can you arrange it?"

The friendly voice answered, "We can dig up a grave within the next three hours. I am the director of the services and you have my word."

"Sounds good to me," answered John and continued without a pause, "I would like him to be buried in a casket."

"You can do that definitely," answered the director. "Select one on your arrival."

"I would be there within the next two hours," was John's response.

After staring at George for a while, John finally said goodbye to him. John extended his arms and lifted George into his chest. While rubbing his back, he whispered into his ear, "In few hours, you will be resting under the ground, separated from me forever."

His mind had to digest what it meant to be without him. The

quiet in the room increased the sense of eternity where he was with George as his companion. The ringing of the phone disrupted the thought process in his mind. The director with the friendly voice was calling.

"Sorry to bother, you left the question of a tombstone unclear. We don't install a stone unless it is asked for."

A tombstone for George was in his head long before he had called the funeral home. He was playing with the idea to have every passerby be aware that the one who rested there was the savior of John. It was the resting place for George, who helped John overcome his illness, was one other way to transmit the idea. He had to come to terms with the words he liked best. He abandoned the idea fast, after realizing that George unfettered him from the chains of a daemon, that was a point, his point, but not a fact, and he was aware of it, and no one else should be drawn into it. His answer to the director was a clear no. "No tombstone."

The question of who George was, especially did he have a mission, dominated his brain again. His easy answer of guardian angel was one way to gratify his mind and it wasn't hard to realize that it satisfied him but wasn't the real answer and didn't throw light on the obscure origin of George. John tried hard to solve the problem to no avail. He called it a day and decided to put his thoughts on a paper and place it in his casket.

To George, who came from nowhere
To help me overcome the alley of despair
The wish to see you again somewhere
Is getting stronger with every passing day

John folded the paper and put it into his breast pocket. Afterwards, he picked up a pillow from the bedroom and placed George on it. His glimpse of it gratified him. It looked like a good spot for George to be transported. The pillow with the lifeless body of George on it laid on the driver seat of his car when he headed toward the funeral home.

While driving, the agonizing thought of George soon lying underground entered his mourning mind. All of a sudden, Jane moved in, reminding him of her part of accommodating George, so the funeral of George should be set in motion by the two of them. He was about to move the car toward Jane's school, but the revival of the cold night bringing George home was the trigger to stay put. *I was the one who brought him in, and I will be the one who puts him under* was his thought and he continued the drive toward the funeral home.

He stopped the car in front of a nondescript building. The two-story structure could pass as a residential home. Doubt took hold of him if it was the right building. His right hand scoured his right pocket and pulled out the address paper, which erased all his second thoughts.

John got off the car and approached the entrance. His eyes were staring at the one foot by one message sign which read, 'Funeral Home for Pets'.

He finally overcame the initial hesitation and opened the door. He faced a wooden counter in the left side of the foyer. It was bare of any decorating objects. A mustached man, with thick black hair showing only streaks of gray, raised from his chair as soon as John came to his sight. His thin face was the big contrast to his protruding belly.

"You must be John. I am Scott, the funeral director, and they shook hands.

John's estimate of his age set him at mid-fifties.

"Follow me this way and you will pass by the coffins you can choose from." John was standing beside the director like a lost man. He was paying attention to what the director was saying, but the image of George lying in the coffin, separated from him, occupied more of his brain.

The director, after a moment, beckoned him to the hallway on the right side of the foyer. The light tossed by a large window on the side of the corridor obviated the need to switch on the light. The shrubbery and a large leafless tree visible through the large window distracted him from the row of caskets on the left side. It was the director who brought his attention back to the caskets by pointing to them. John's head turned to the coffins. His gloomy eyes were testimony to his grief that soon George will be lying in one of them and be separated from him forever. At the same time, his eyes couldn't separate from an oak wood coffin just two steps away. Scott, who was watching him closely, moved a step ahead and said, "Let me show you the inside."

As he lifted the top, a thick layer of blackish velvet, covering the top and the bottom of the casket, revealed itself to the onlooker. John pressed his index and middle fingers against the velvet. The deep indentation proved to him its thickness and softness.

After a glance at the director, John's mouth opened and he uttered, "Well, I will take this one."

The fast decision of John made Scott's lips take up the crescent shape. "Let me have Ross bring it to your car and guide you to the cemetery."

"I prefer a private funeral," jumped out of John's mouth. "Just tell him to bring it to my car and give me the direction to the cemetery. The only person present at the funeral would be me. Remember, you promised the grave would ready by the time I arrive."

Scott had a hard time avoiding the disbelief in his eyes. How can anybody refuse his generous offer of providing guidance to the cemetery? He responded with a low voice, "As you wish."

Scott started scribbling the direction of the cemetery on a piece of paper and handed it over to John when he was done.

John shook hands with him and said, "I appreciate your efforts, send me the bill," and left.

The directions lead to a parking lot which loomed after a five-minute drive. Short of a red Corolla, which was parked in the first row, the lot was empty.

John parked just few steps away from the grave site. He lifted George's body carefully, opened the trunk and placed it into the coffin. He meticulously studied the piece of paper on which Scott had outlined the grave site. He buried his concern. Where he had parked was not far away from the burial site, about hundred yards away, and to carry the coffin with George inside it required the services of both of his arms.

Maple trees were planted densely on the north side of the cemetery where John stood, holding the coffin. The cold pierced through his clothes and he felt the heaviness of the casket, making him wish he hadn't eschewed Scott's offer. After a few minutes of walking, he realized the coffin was wearing on him, but fortunately his eyes caught the sight of piled up earth. He put down the coffin and checked the paper Scott had scribbled for him. The stockpile of soil matched the grave site. Carrying the coffin with both arms, he walked slowly toward it. He passed by an old couple who were standing hand in hand, their eyes fixed at a tombstone. John's arms tightened, his steps grew faster until he was just few steps away from the dug earth.

A young man sitting on an unfolded chair, his hands wrapped around a spate handle with the blade resting on the ground, got up as soon as he saw John and said, "Hi, my name is Tony, and I dug up the grave and will help you to put the coffin inside."

John, who had placed the coffin at the grave site, was slightly short of breath; obviously, he had overestimated his physical strength when he stepped up his pace while carrying the casket. He expressed his thanks and lifted up the coffin lid. The sight of lifeless George encircled by a black velvet froze him. After having his composure back, he pulled out his note on George and read it again, 'to George, who came from nowhere', though he had read it three times. He finally folded and placed it on the right side of George's head and, with a heavy heart, slowly brought the lid down.

Tony and he lowered the casket toward the ground of the grave until it was resting on the cold soil.

A film of moisture blurred John's last look of it. He beckoned Tony to fill up the grave, while his eyes were alternating between the grave being filled up and the pile of soil diminishing in size.

When the pile of soil vanished and the grave became level with the grass, John shook hand with Tony and expressed his thanks.

CHAPTER TWENTY-THREE

Once inside the car, he fastened his security belt and pushed the fifth of Mahler into the CD player. It had never hit his mind that the day will come when he would be listening to the funeral march of Mahler's fifth symphony right after George's funeral.

Through the windshield, he watched the leafless branches of the maple trees which were showing him the direction of the wind. The clouds were dark and very low. The cemetery had assumed an abandoned look, which reminded him of the old couple whom he passed by. The red Corolla was gone – obviously it was their car.

The wetness in his eyes was increasing. He moved his right arm to wipe them before turning on the engine.

The middle path of the parking lead him to the highway which headed toward his neighborhood. The funeral march was vibrating in the air. That is when the idea of a home devoid of George's accompaniment crept into his mind and took his gloomy mood a notch higher. He didn't hear the loud honking of a passing driver. It was conceivable that he was totally absent-minded behind the wheel. Whatever the cause, he wasn't taking note of other road users, who mostly swerved and passed. Even showing the finger while passing didn't make him aware of how slow he was on a major highway. His thoughts were focused on the coffin lying deep in the ground with his beloved George while Mahler's funeral march sounded in the air.

He had set the temperature in the car at seventy, but he felt cold and was sweating, and tried to wipe the cold sweat on his neck with the palm of his right hand, while the pain in his left arm, radiating to his left jaw, became so intense that he pulled over the car to the shoulder. The pain became intensified and he put his head on the steering wheel. As soon as his face had touched the wheel, his pain disappeared and the calmness returned to him. He was no more in the car, but floating in the air, glancing at the lifeless body of John with his head on the wheel. He looked around, the sky, the highway; the cars were gone and everywhere he glanced at was light, light of indescribable and stunning beauty. He thought he was floating but indeed he had become part of the light, and could be anywhere at no time.

When he focused, he figured out faces and bodies in the light and, at closer look, they appeared to have human shape. He focused and recognized George's face and he thought he saw wings spreading from his side. That is when all his fairy tale figures with wings appeared, moving as part of the light toward him. When they closed in on him, he could distinguish without a doubt George's face, with two dark eyes among them. Even though he was part of the light, the expression on his face read, "This time I will stay with you, forever."